The Sea, Ships and Sailors

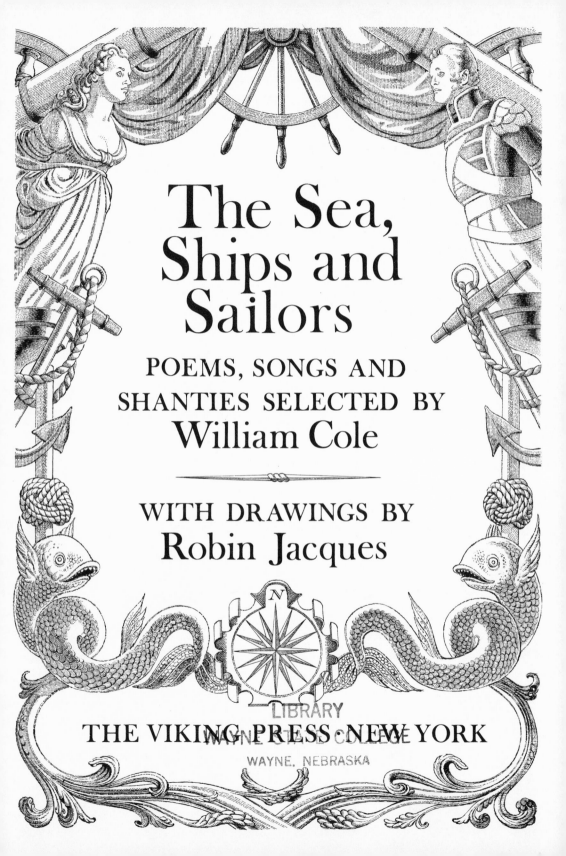

The Sea, Ships and Sailors

POEMS, SONGS AND
SHANTIES SELECTED BY
William Cole

WITH DRAWINGS BY
Robin Jacques

THE VIKING PRESS · NEW YORK

Text Copyright © 1967 by William Cole
Illustrations Copyright © 1967 by Robin Jacques
All rights reserved
First published in 1967 by The Viking Press, Inc.
625 Madison Avenue, New York, N.Y. 10022
Published simultaneously in Canada by
The Macmillan Company of Canada Limited

Library of Congress catalog card number: 67–24856
Printed in U.S.A. by Murray Printing
808.81   1. Poetry—Collections
              2. Sea poetry

ACKNOWLEDGMENTS

Acknowledgment is made to the following for permission to use material owned by them. Every reasonable effort has been made to clear the use of the poems in this volume with copyright owners. If notified of any omissions, the editor and publisher will gladly make the proper corrections in future editions.

A. D. Peters & Co., for "Rousecastle" by David Wright.
Alfred A. Knopf, Inc., for "Winter Ocean" from *Telephone Poles* by John Updike. © Copyright 1960 by John Updike.
Appleton-Century, Inc., affiliate of Meredith Press, for "Noah an' Jonah an' Cap'n John Smith" from *Noah an' Jonah an' Cap'n John Smith* by Don Marquis. Copyright 1921 by D. Appleton & Co., Copyright renewed, 1949 by Don Marquis.
The Ben Roth Agency Inc., for "The Albatross" by R. P. Lister. © Punch Publications Ltd.
Chatto & Windus Ltd. and Mrs. Laura Huxley, for "Jonah" by Aldous Huxley from *Verses and a Comedy*.
Doubleday & Company, Inc. and Mrs. George Bambridge, for "Mulholland's Contract" from *Rudyard Kipling's Verse: Definitive Edition*.
E. P. Dutton & Co., Inc., for "A Long Time Ago," "The Gals o' Dublin Town," "Blow, Ye Winds," "Haul Away Joe," and "The Chinee Bumboatman" from the book *Shanties from the Seven Seas* compiled by Stan Hugill. Copyright © 1961 by Stan Hugill; "The Sea" from the book *The Wandering Moon* by James Reeves. Published 1960 by E. P. Dutton & Co., Inc.
Indiana University Press, for "The Circus Ship *Euzkera*" by Walker Gibson from *The Reckless Spenders*.
J. B. Lippincott Company, for "Old Gray Squirrel" from *Collected Poems* by Alfred Noyes. Copyright 1920, 1948 by Alfred Noyes.
The Literary Trustees of Walter de la Mare and The Society of Authors as their representative, for "Sam" by Walter de la Mare.
Macmillan & Co. Ltd., London, and Mr. Michael Gibson, for "Flannan Isle" and "Luck" from *Collected Poems* by Wilfrid Gibson.
The Macmillan Company, New York, for "An Inscription by the Sea" from *Collected Poems* by E. A. Robinson. Copyright 1915 by Edwin Arlington Robinson. Renewed 1943 by Ruth Nivison; "The Yarn of the *Loch Achray*" and "Cape Horn Gospel" from *Poems* by J. Masefield. Published 1913 by The Macmillan Company. Renewed 1944 by John Masefield; "Cargoes," "Captain Stratton's Fancy," and "Sea Fever" from *Poems* by J. Masefield. Copyright 1912 by The Macmillan Company. Renewed 1940 by John Masefield; "A Ballad of John Silver" from *Salt Water Ballads* by John Mase-

field. Copyright 1916 by John Masefield. Renewed 1944 by John Masefield.

The Marchesa Origo, for "Frutta di Mare" from *Poems* by Geoffrey Scott.

Oxford University Press, London, for "The Ballad of *Kon-Tiki*" by Ian Serraillier from *The Ballad of* Kon-Tiki *and Other Verses.*

Pegasus Press Ltd., for "The Anchorage" by Pat Wilson from *The Bright Sea.*

Routledge & Kegan Paul Ltd., for "Wind, Waves and Sails" by M. La Rue from *Poems by Children 1950–1961* edited by Michael Baldwin.

The Ryerson Press, Toronto, for "The Wreckers' Prayer" from *The Leather Bottle* by Theodore Goodridge Roberts.

Sidgwick & Jackson Ltd. and the author's representatives, for "Fog" from *Vagabond Verses* by Crosbie Garstin.

Shel Silverstein, for his poem "The Silver Fish."

William Jay Smith, for his poem "The Waves."

William Morris Agency, Inc., for "Sea Chanty" by Abe Burrows. Copyright © 1955 by Abram S. Burrows.

Contents

Introduction

Poets have always been drawn to the sea; the sea is adventure, mystery, beauty, violence. It is the totally unconquerable force. It feeds us and it drowns us. It still contains, in its deeps, living creatures no man has ever seen. And I don't mean mermaids.

There is much less sea poetry being written today than there was in the old days of sailing ships, pirates, slavers, and picturesque adventurers. There's nothing really romantic about an ocean liner or an oil tanker; their destinations may be romantic, but getting there is usually as uneventful as a game of shuffleboard. Not so way back in the days of sail, when it could take months to get from Europe to America; when vessels had to fight their way around the Horn; when an approaching ship might suddenly hoist the Jolly Roger on you—*there's* the stuff of poetry! The gnarled old sea dog who sits whittling on the dock and spinning yarns has disappeared. Today's sailor on leave, in his civvy clothes, could be mistaken for a salesman or an off-duty policeman. He doesn't know any yarns, really, and he couldn't tell a shanty from a shoehorn. There is no more "adventuring"; things are done by radio and radar. Ships seldom get lost, and there are few shipwrecks. And *should* there be a ship-wreck—somewhere in the South Seas—it would be difficult to find an unpopulated desert island to get cast away on—and what fun is a ship-wreck without a desert island?

But we can be thankful for the romantic tales we've had, and put our-selves back in those times and take part in such dashing stories as Brown-ing's "Hervé Riel" and Masefield's "The Yarn of the *Loch Achray*." Contemporary adventuring on the sea is pretty much confined to the sort of voyage described in Ian Serrallier's "The Ballad of the *Kon-Tiki*."

In reading sea poems until I felt I had water on the brain, I was surprised to find that so many are humorous. Poets seem always to have thought that there was something inherently funny about a pirate chief, an ec-centric skipper, or a yarning sailor. Exaggeration, of course, is an essential ingredient of humor: I dare say that meeting a pirate chief in his natural habitat would be the opposite of funny; that sailing-ship skippers weren't lovable eccentrics but pretty tough birds, and that *any* yarning sailor would soon become a bore. But what fun the exaggerations are: Wallace Irwin's skipper who says, "Ain't I supposed to skip?" the jolly jack-tars of W. S. Gilbert, and the ridiculous parody of a shanty by Abe Burrows, with the haunting refrain: "Poop the deck,/ Beat the breeze . . . Pepper the mints,/ We're sailing away on the sea."

Speaking on shanties: Most do not come over well as poems. They were work songs (shanty, from the French word *chanter*, "to sing"), and had oft-repeated refrains which were sung to coordinate the rhythm of hauling and pushing—work that is now done quietly by machines. But there are, of course, many marvelous sea songs, and some—those that read well as poems—are in this book. If you want to hear them sung—with real gusto—listen to the records of The Clancy Brothers and Tommy Makem. They have a particularly fine time with that looney song "The *Irish Rover*."

There is fantastic variety to the sea, and I have tried in this collection to

8

represent all its moods. The sea is hurricanes and lullabies, gaiety and doom, crashing surf and quiet depths. It is, above all—the word I used earlier—unconquerable. Joseph Conrad, a great writer who spent many years at sea, wrote: "Faithful to no race after the manner of the kindly earth, receiving no impression from valor and toil and self-sacrifice, recognizing no finality of dominion, the sea has never adopted the cause of its masters like the land."

WILLIAM COLE

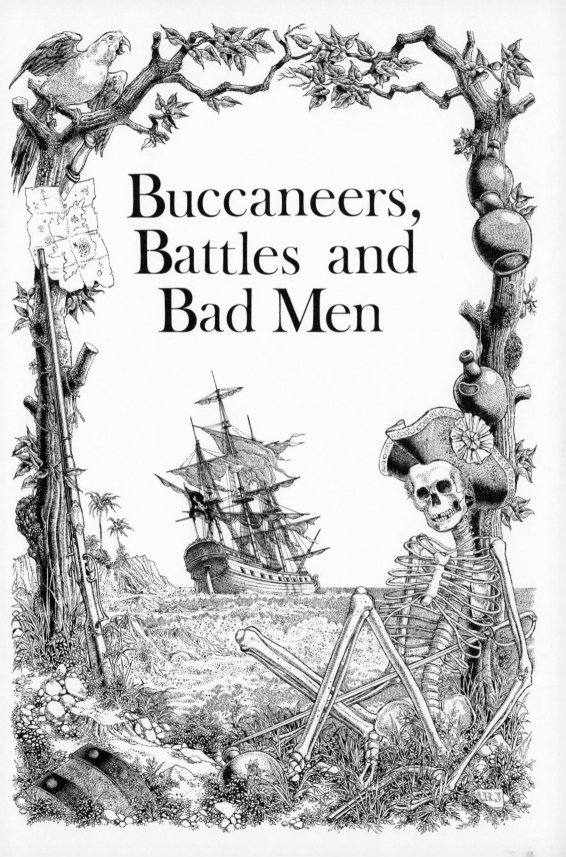

Buccaneers, Battles and Bad Men

A Ballad
of John Silver

We were schooner-rigged and rakish, with a long and lissome hull,
And we flew the pretty colors of the crossbones and the skull;
We'd a big black Jolly Roger flapping grimly at the fore,
And we sailed the Spanish Water in the happy days of yore.

We'd a long brass gun amidships, like a well-conducted ship,
We had each a brace of pistols and a cutlass at the hip;
It's a point which tells against us, and a fact to be deplored,
But we chased the goodly merchantmen and laid their ships aboard.

Then the dead men fouled the scuppers and the wounded filled the chains,
And the paint-work all was spatter-dashed with other people's brains.
She was boarded, she was looted, she was scuttled till she sank,
And the pale survivors left us by the medium of the plank.

O! then it was (while standing by the taffrail on the poop)
We could hear the drowning folk lament the absent chicken coop;
Then, having washed the blood away, we'd little else to do
Than to dance a quiet hornpipe as the old salts taught us to.

O! the fiddle on the fo'c's'le, and the slapping naked soles,
And the genial "Down the middle, Jake, and curtsy when she rolls!"
With the silver seas around us and the pale moon overhead,
And the lookout not a-looking and his pipe bowl glowing red.

Ah! the pig-tailed, quidding pirates and the pretty pranks we played,
All have since been put a stop to by the naughty Board of Trade;
The schooners and the merry crews are laid away to rest,
A little south the sunset in the Islands of the Blest.

JOHN MASEFIELD

Little Billee

There were three sailors of Bristol city
Who took a boat and went to sea.
But first with beef and captain's biscuits
And pickled pork they loaded she.

There was gorging Jack and guzzling Jimmy,
And the youngest he was little Bill-ee.
Now, when they got as far as the equator
They'd nothing left but one split pea.

Says gorging Jack to guzzling Jimmy,
"I am extremely hungaree."
To gorging Jack says guzzling Jimmy,
"We've nothing left, we must eat we."

Says gorging Jack to guzzling Jimmy,
"With one another we shouldn't agree!
There's little Bill, he's young and tender,
We're old and tough, so let's eat he.

"Oh, Billy, we're going to kill and eat you,
So undo the button of your chemie."
When Bill received this information
He used his pocket handkerchie.

"First let me say my catechism,
Which my poor mammy taught to me."
"Make haste, make haste," says guzzling Jimmy,
While Jack pulled out his snickersnee.

So Billy went up to the main-top gallant mast,
And down he fell on his bended knee.
He scarce had come to the Twelfth Commandment
When up he jumps. "There's land I see:

"Jerusalem and Madagascar,
And North and South Amerikee:
There's the British flag a-riding at anchor,
With Admiral Napier, K.C.B."

So when they got aboard of the Admiral's,
He hanged fat Jack and flogged Jimmee:
But as for little Bill, he made him
The Captain of a Seventy-three.

WILLIAM MAKEPEACE THACKERAY

Derelict

This is a poem based on a four-line fragment in Robert Louis Stevenson's Treasure Island. *The* Dead Man's Chest *is a dangerous hidden reef in the Caribbean Sea. The legend is that a rich Spanish galleon was seized by pirates, who fought among themselves over the loot. Fifteen of them set their companions adrift, and then, of course, fought again among* themselves. *All died, and the boat drifted onto the Dead Man's Chest. It was subsequently discovered by the men in the boat that had been set adrift. Here is what they found:*

>Fifteen men on the Dead Man's Chest—
>Drink and the devil had done for the rest—
>The mate was fixed by the bo's'n's pike,
>The bo's'n brained with a marline spike,
>And Cookey's throat was marked belike.
>It had been gripped
>By fingers ten;
>And there they lay,
>All good, dead men,
>Like break-o'-day in a boozing ken—
>Yo-ho-ho and a bottle of rum!

Fifteen men of a whole ship's list—
Dead and be-damned and the rest gone whist!—
   The skipper lay with his nob in gore
   Where the scullion's axe his cheek had shore—
   And the scullion he was stabbed times four.
      And there they lay,
         And the soggy skies
      Dripped all day long
         In up-staring eyes—
At murk sunset and at foul sunrise—
   Yo-ho-ho and a bottle of rum!

Fifteen men of 'em stiff and stark—
Ten of the crew had the murder mark—
   'Twas a cutlass swipe, or an ounce of lead,
   Or a yawing hole in a battered head—
   And the scuppers glut with a rotting red.
      And there they lay—
         Aye, damn my eyes!—
      All lookouts clapped
         On paradise—
All souls bound just contrariwise—
   Yo-ho-ho and a bottle of rum!

Fifteen men of 'em good and true—
Every man jack could ha' sailed with Old Pew—
   There was chest on chest full of Spanish gold,
   With a ton of plate in the middle hold,
   And the cabins, riot of loot untold.
      And they lay there
         That had took the plum,

With sightless glare
          And their lips struck dumb,
While we shared all by the rule of thumb—
     Yo-ho-ho and a bottle of rum!

Fifteen men on the Dead Man's Chest—
Drink and the devil had done for the rest—
     We wrapped 'em all in a mains'l tight,
     With twice ten turns of a hawser's bight,
     And we heaved 'em over and out of sight—
          With a yo-heave-ho!
          And a fare-you-well!
     And a sullen plunge
          In the sullen swell,
Ten fathoms deep on the road to hell!
     Yo-ho-ho and a bottle of rum!

YOUNG EWING ALLISON

The Post Captain

When they heard the Captain humming and beheld the dancing crew,
On the *Royal Biddy* frigate was Sir Peter Bombazoo;
His mind was full of music and his head was full of tunes,
And he cheerfully exhibited on pleasant afternoons.

He could whistle, on his fingers, an invigorating reel,
And could imitate a piper on the handles of the wheel;
He could play in double octaves, too, all up and down the rail,
Or rattle off a rondo on the bottom of a pail.

Then porters with their packages and bakers with their buns,
And countesses in carriages and grenadiers with guns,
And admirals and commodores arrived from near and far,
To listen to the music of this entertaining tar.

When they heard the Captain humming and beheld the dancing crew,
The commodores severely said, "Why, this will never do!"

And the admirals all hurried home, remarking, "This is most
Extraordinary conduct for a captain at his post."

Then they sent some sailing orders to Sir Peter, in a boat,
And he did a little fifing on the edges of the note;
But he read the sailing orders, as of course he had to do,
And removed the *Royal Biddy* to the Bay of Boohgabooh.

Now, Sir Peter took it kindly, but it's proper to explain
He was sent to catch a pirate out upon the Spanish Main.
And he played, with variations, an imaginary tune
On the buttons of his waistcoat, like a jocular bassoon.

Then a topman saw the Pirate come a-sailing in the bay,
And reported to the Captain in the ordinary way.
"I'll receive him," said Sir Peter, "with a musical salute,"
And he gave some imitations of a double-jointed flute.

Then the Pirate cried derisively, "I've heard it done before!"
And he hoisted up a banner emblematical of gore.
But Sir Peter said serenely, "You may double-shot the guns
While I sing my little ballad of 'The Butter on the Buns.' "

Then the Pirate banged Sir Peter and Sir Peter banged him back,
And they banged away together as they took another tack.
Then Sir Peter said, politely, "You may board him, if you like,"
And he played a little dirge upon the handle of a pike.

Then the "Biddies" poured like hornets down upon the Pirate's deck
And Sir Peter caught the Pirate and he took him by the neck,
And remarked, "You must excuse me, but you acted like a brute
When I gave my imitation of that double-jointed flute."

So they took that wicked Pirate and they took his wicked crew,
And tied them up with double knots in packages of two,
And left them lying on their backs in rows upon the beach
With a little bread and water within comfortable reach.

Now the Pirate had a treasure (mostly silverware and gold),
And Sir Peter took and stowed it in the bottom of his hold;
And said, "I will retire on this cargo of doubloons,
And each of you, my gallant crew, may have some silver spoons."

Now commodores in coach-and-fours and corporals in cabs,
And men with carts of pies and tarts and fishermen with crabs,
And barristers with wigs, in gigs, still gather on the strand,
But there isn't any music save a little German band.

CHARLES EDWARD CARRYL

The Old Navy

The captain stood on the carronade: "First Lieutenant," says he,
"Send all my merry men aft here, for they must list to me;
I haven't the gift of the gab, my sons—because I'm bred to the sea;
That ship there is a Frenchman, who means to fight with we.
    And odds bobs, hammer and tongs, long as I've been to sea,
    I've fought 'gainst every odds—but I've gained the victory!

"That ship there is a Frenchman, and if we don't take she,
'Tis a thousand bullets to one, that she will capture we;
I haven't the gift of the gab, my boys; so each man to his gun;
If she's not mine in half an hour, I'll flog each mother's son.
    For odds bobs, hammer and tongs, long as I've been to sea,
    I've fought 'gainst every odds—and I've gained the victory!"

We fought for twenty minutes, when the Frenchman had enough;
"I little thought," said he, "that your men were of such stuff."
Our captain took the Frenchman's sword, a low bow made to he;
"I haven't the gift of the gab, monsieur, but polite I wish to be.
   And odds bobs, hammer and tongs, long as I've been to sea,
   I've fought 'gainst every odds—and I've gained the victory!"

Our captain sent for all of us: "My merry men," said he,
"I haven't the gift of the gab, my lads, but yet I thankful be;
You've done your duty handsomely, each man stood to his gun;
If you hadn't, you villians, as sure as day, I'd have flogged each mother's son,
   For odds bobs, hammer and tongs, as long as I'm at sea,
   I'll fight 'gainst every odds—and I'll gain the victory!"

FREDERICK MARRYAT

El Capitan-General

There was a captain-general who ruled in Vera Cruz,
And what we used to hear of him was always evil news:
He was a pirate on the sea—a robber on the shore,
The Señor Don Alonzo Estabán San Salvador.

There was a Yankee skipper who round about did roam;
His name was Stephen Folger, and Nantucket was his home:
And having gone to Vera Cruz, he had been skinned full sore
By the Señor Don Alonzo Estabán San Salvador.

But having got away alive, though all his cash was gone,
He said, "If there is vengeance, I will surely try it on!
And I do wish I may be damned if I don't clear the score
With Señor Don Alonzo Estabán San Salvador!"

He shipped a crew of seventy men—well armèd men were they,
And sixty of them in the hold he darkly stowed away;
And, sailing back to Vera Cruz, was sighted from the shore
By the Señor Don Alonzo Estabán San Salvador.

With twenty-five *soldados* he came on board so pleased,
And said, "*Maldito* Yankee—again your ship is seized.
How many sailors have you got?" Said Folger, "Ten—no more,"
To the Captain Don Alonzo Estabán San Salvador.

"But come into my cabin and take a glass of wine.
I do suppose, as usual, I'll have to pay a fine:
I have got some old Madeira, and we'll talk the matter o'er—
My Captain Don Alonzo Estabán San Salvador."

And as over that Madeira the captain-general boozed,
It seemed to him as if his head was getting quite confused;
For it happened that some morphine had traveled from the store
To the glass of Don Alonzo Estabán San Salvador.

"What is it makes the vessel roll? What sounds are these I hear?
It seems as if the rising waves were beating on my ear!"
"Oh, it is the breaking of the surf—just that and nothing more,
My Captain Don Alonzo Estabán San Salvador!"

The governor was in a sleep which muddled all his brains;
The seventy men had got his gang and put them all in chains;
And when he woke the following day he could not see the shore,
For he was out on the blue water—the Don San Salvador.

"Now do you see that yardarm—and understand the thing?"
Said Captain Folger. "For all from that yardarm you shall swing,
Or forty thousand dollars you shall pay me from your store,
My Captain Don Alonzo Estabán San Salvador."

The Capitano took a pen—the order he did sign—
"O Señor Yankee! but you charge amazing high for wine!"
But 'twas not till the draft was paid they let him go ashore,
El Señor Don Alonzo Estabán San Salvador.

The greatest sharp some day will find another sharper wit;
It always makes the Devil laugh to see a biter bit;
It takes two Spaniards any day to come a Yankee o'er—
Even two like Don Alonzo Estabán San Salvador.

CHARLES GODFREY LELAND

The Ballad
of the *Billycock*

It was the good ship *Billycock,* with thirteen men aboard,
  Athirst to grapple with their country's foes—
A crew, 'twill be admitted, not numerically fitted
  To navigate a battleship in prose.

It was the good ship *Billycock* put out from Plymouth Sound,
  While lustily the gallant heroes cheered,
And all the air was ringing with the merry bo'sun's singing,
  Till in the gloom of night she disappeared.

But when the morning broke on her, behold, a dozen ships,
  A dozen ships of France, around her lay
(Or if that isn't plenty, I will gladly make it twenty),
  And hemmed her close in Salamander Bay.

Then to the Lord High Admiral there spake a cabin boy;
  "Methinks," he said, "the odds are somewhat great,
And, in the present crisis, a cabin boy's advice is
  That you and France had better arbitrate."

"Pooh!" said the Lord High Admiral, and slapped his lordly chest,
  "Pooh! that would be both cowardly and wrong;
Shall I, a gallant fighter, give the needy ballad writer
  No suitable material for song?

"Nay—is the shorthand writer here? I tell you, one and all,
  I mean to do my duty as I ought;
With eager satisfaction let us clear the decks for action
  And fight the craven Frenchmen!" So they fought.

And (after several stanzas which as yet are incomplete,
  Describing all the fight in epic style)
When the *Billycock* was going, she'd a dozen prizes towing
  (Or twenty, as above) in single file.

Ah, long in glowing English hearts the story will remain,
  The memory of that historic day,
And, while we rule the ocean, we will picture with emotion
  The *Billycock* in Salamander Bay!

P. S. I've lately noticed that the critics, who, I think,
  In praising *my* productions are remiss—
Quite easily are captured, and profess themselves enraptured,
  By patriotic ditties such as this.

For making which you merely take some dauntless Englishmen,
  Guns, heroism, slaughter and a fleet—

Ingredients you mingle in a meter with a jingle,
　　And there you have your masterpiece complete.

Why, then, with labor infinite, produce a book of verse,
　　To languish on the "All at Twopence" shelf?
The ballad bold and breezy comes particularly easy—
　　I mean to take to writing it myself!

ANTHONY C. DEANE

O'er the Wild
Gannet's Bath

O'er the wild gannet's bath
Come the Norse coursers!
O'er the whale's heritance
Gloriously steering!
With beaked heads peering,
Deep-plunging, high-rearing,
Tossing their foam abroad,
Shaking white manes aloft,
Creamy-neck'd, pitchy-ribb'd,
Steeds of the ocean!

O'er the Sun's mirror green
Come the Norse coursers!
Trampling its glassy breadth
Into bright fragments!

Hollow-back'd, huge-bosom'd,
Fraught with mail'd riders,
Clanging with hauberks,
Shield, spear, and battleaxe,
Canvas-wing'd, cable-rein'd,
Steeds of the Ocean!

O'er the Wind's ploughing field
Come the Norse coursers!
By a hundred each ridden,
To the bloody feast bidden,
They rush in their fierceness
And ravine all round them!
Their shoulders enriching
With fleecy-light plunder,
Fire-spreading, foe-spurning,
Steeds of the Ocean!

GEORGE DARLEY

The Battle

of Clothesline Bay

The neatest officer on the coast—
   Hang your sails to the whiffletree slat!—
Was the famous Admiral Buttertoast
   Who sailed the historical *Derby Hat*.
Flutter the ensign, whittle the screw
For the neat old Admiral and his crew!

His sailormen were the tidiest tars
   That sought renown 'neath the billowing flags

As they stood in place on the decks and spars
    With carpet sweepers and dusting rags.
And Monday mornings the sails they'd reef
And iron 'em out like a handkerchief.

"Men," said the Admiral, "I abhor
    To litter my boat with the shot and shell,
And it's very untidy to go to war
    And scent my sails with the powder smell;
So load the cannon with scouring soap
And sachet powder of heliotrope."

About this period on the main
    Sailed the slatternly pirate, Grimy Dan,
Whose slipshod methods were terribly plain
    In the state of his vessel, the *Frying Pan,*
Where the decks were littered with bottles and crumbs
And the masts were smeared by his gory thumbs.

So the grim marauders of Grimy Dan
    Sailed the greasy *Frying Pan* into the bay
Where the *Derby Hat* all spick and span
    A-drying her clothes in the offing lay.
"Ho!" cried the Pirate, and likewise, "Hum!
Edam Schnapps and Jamaica Rum!

"By me bloody yards and me slippery plank,
    What is the scent from yon vessel blown?"
"That," quoth the bo's'n, Terrible Hank,
    "Is washing powder and eau de cologne."
"Heave-ho, mateys," said Dan, "and away!
I risk no battles on washing day."

"Friends," said the Admiral, "I confess
    I'm glad to be rid of the rude galoots.
They might have caused a terrible mess
    By tracking our decks with their muddy boots.
Dear me suds! what a shock it would be
To a shipshape, housekeeping man like me!"

So the *Frying Pan* with her tattered crew
    Like a dingy specter slunk from the scene
And the Admiral neat, when the foe withdrew,
    Sent a wireless telegram to his Queen,
"I beg to report, if your Majesty please,
I have lathered the Pirates and scoured the seas."

WALLACE IRWIN

Captain Stratton's Fancy

Oh, some are fond of red wine, and some are fond of white,
And some are all for dancing by the pale moonlight;
But rum alone's the tipple, and the heart's delight
   Of the old bold mate of Henry Morgan.

Oh, some are fond of Spanish wine, and some are fond of French,
And some'll swallow tay and stuff fit only for a wench;
But I'm for right Jamaica till I roll beneath the bench,
   Says the old bold mate of Henry Morgan.

Oh, some are for the lily, and some are for the rose,
But I am for the sugar cane that in Jamaica grows;
For it's that that makes the bonny drink to warm my copper nose,
   Says the old bold mate of Henry Morgan.

Oh, some are fond of fiddles, and a song well sung,
And some are all for music for to lilt upon the tongue;
But mouths were made for tankards, and for sucking at the bung,
    Says the old bold mate of Henry Morgan.

Oh, some are fond of dancing, and some are fond of dice,
And some are all for red lips, and pretty lasses' eyes;
But a right Jamaica puncheon is a finer prize
    To the old bold mate of Henry Morgan.

Oh, some that's good and godly ones they hold that it's a sin
To troll the jolly bowl around, and let the dollars spin;
But I'm for toleration and for drinking at an inn,
    Says the old bold mate of Henry Morgan.

Oh, some are sad and wretched folk that go in silken suits,
And there's a mort of wicked rogues that live in good reputes;
So I'm for drinking honestly, and dying in my boots,
    Like an old bold mate of Henry Morgan.

JOHN MASEFIELD

The Moods
of the Sea

Winter Ocean

Many-maned scud-thumper, tub
of many whales, maker of worn wood, shrub-
ruster, sky-mocker, rave!
portly pusher of waves, wind-slave.

JOHN UPDIKE

Fog

Over the oily swell it heaved, it rolled,
    Like some foul creature, filmy, nebulous.
It pushed out streaming tentacles, took clammy hold,
Swaddled the spars, wrapped us in damp and cold,
    Blotted the sun, crept round and over us.

Day long, night long, it hid us from the sky—
    Hid us from sun and stars as in a tomb.
Shrouded in mist a berg went groaning by.
Far and forlorn we heard the blind ships cry
    Like lost souls wailing in a hopeless gloom.

Like a bellwether clanging from the fold,
    A codder called her dories. With scared breath
The steamer sirens shrieked; and mad bells tolled.
Through time eternal in the dark we rolled
    Playing a game of Blind-Man's-Buff with Death.

CROSBIE GARSTIN

The Sands of Dee

"O Mary, go and call the cattle home,
    And call the cattle home,
    And call the cattle home
  Across the sands of Dee";
The western wind was wild and dank with foam,
  And all alone went she.

The western tide crept up along the sand,
    And o'er and o'er the sand,
    And round and round the sand,
  As far as eye could see.
The rolling mist came down and hid the land:
  And never home came she.

"Oh! is it weed, or fish, or floating hair—
    A tress of golden hair,
    A drowned maiden's hair
  Above the nets at sea?

Was never salmon yet that shone so fair
    Among the stakes on Dee."

They rowed her in across the rolling foam,
    The cruel crawling foam,
    The cruel hungry foam,
  To her grave beside the sea:
But still the boatmen hear her call the cattle home
    Across the sands of Dee.

CHARLES KINGSLEY

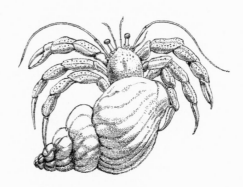

The Waves

The waves that come down from the edge of the sky
    Descend the green sea-lanes;
Up from the green the white gulls fly,
    And the fish like monoplanes.

O the sky's an umbrella of sea-blue air
    With a handle brightly pearled;
It opens up on everywhere,
    It opens on the world.

The waves that come down from the edge of the sky
    On the edge of evening break.
Our Lord the Peacock walks on high,
    The heavens in His wake.

WILLIAM JAY SMITH

The Ocean

(from *Childe Harold*)

There is a pleasure in the pathless woods,
There is a rapture on the lonely shore,
There is society, where none intrudes,
By the deep Sea, and music in its roar:
I love not Man the less, but Nature more,
From these our interviews, in which I steal
From all I may be, or have been before,
To mingle with the Universe, and feel
What I can ne'er express, yet cannot all conceal.

Roll on, thou deep and dark blue Ocean—roll!
Ten thousand fleets sweep over thee in vain;
Man marks the earth with ruin—his control
Stops with the shore; upon the watery plain
The wrecks are all thy deed, nor doth remain
A shadow of man's ravage, save his own,
When, for a moment, like a drop of rain,
He sinks into thy depths with bubbling groan,
Without a grave, unknelled, uncoffined and unknown. . . .

Thy shores are empires, changed in all save thee—
Assyria, Greece, Rome, Carthage, what are they?
Thy waters washed them power while they were free,
And many a tyrant since; their shores obey
The stranger, slave or savage; their decay
Has dried up realms to deserts:—not so thou;
Unchangeable, save to thy wild waves' play,
Time writes no wrinkle on thine azure brow:
Such as creation's dawn beheld, thou rollest now.

And I have loved thee, Ocean! and my joy
Of youthful sports was on thy breast to be
Borne, like thy bubbles, onward: from a boy
I wanton'd with thy breakers—they to me
Were a delight; and if the freshening sea
Made them a terror—'twas a pleasing fear,
For I was as it were a child of thee,
And trusted to thy billows far and near,
And laid my hand upon thy mane—as I do here.

GEORGE GORDON, LORD BYRON

A Cradle Song

Sweet and low, sweet and low,
   Wind of the western sea,
Low, low, breathe and blow,
   Wind of the western sea!
Over the rolling waters go,
Come from the dying moon, and blow,
   Blow him again to me;
While my little one, while my pretty one, sleeps.

Sleep and rest, sleep and rest,
   Father will come to thee soon;
Rest, rest, on Mother's breast,
   Father will come to thee soon;
Father will come to his babe in the nest,
Silver sails all out of the west,
   Under the silver moon:
Sleep, my little one, sleep, my pretty one, sleep.

ALFRED, LORD TENNYSON

After the Sea Ship

After the sea ship, after the whistling winds,
After the white-gray sails taut to their spars and ropes,
Below, a myriad myriad waves hastening, lifting up their necks,
Tending in ceaseless flow toward the track of the ship,
Waves of the ocean bubbling and gurgling, blithely prying,
Waves, undulating waves, liquid, uneven, emulous waves,
Toward that whirling current, laughing and buoyant, with curves,
Where the great vessel sailing and tacking displaced the surface,
Larger and smaller waves in the spread of the ocean yearnfully flowing,
The wake of the sea ship after she passes, flashing and frolicsome under the sun,
A motley procession with many a fleck of foam and many fragments,
Following the stately and rapid ship, in the wake following.

WALT WHITMAN

49

The Tide Rises,
the Tide Falls

The tide rises, the tide falls,
The twilight darkens, the curlew calls;
Along the sea-sands damp and brown
The traveler hastens toward the town;
    And the tide rises, the tide falls.

Darkness settles on roofs and walls,
But the sea in the darkness calls and calls;
The little waves, with their soft white hands,
Efface the footprints in the sands,
    And the tide rises, the tide falls.

The morning breaks; the steeds in their stalls
Stamp and neigh, as the hostler calls;
The day returns; but nevermore
Returns the traveler to the shore,
    And the tide rises, the tide falls.

HENRY WADSWORTH LONGFELLOW

The Sea

The sea is a hungry dog,
Giant and gray.
He rolls on the beach all day.
With his clashing teeth and shaggy jaws

Hour upon hour he gnaws
The rumbling, tumbling stones,
And "Bones, bones, bones, bones!"
The giant sea-dog moans,
Licking his greasy paws.

And when the night wind roars
And the moon rocks in the stormy cloud,
He bounds to his feet and snuffs and sniffs,
Shaking his wet sides over the cliffs,
And howls and hollos long and loud.

But on quiet days in May or June,
When even the grasses on the dune
Play no more their reedy tune,
With his head between his paws
He lies on the sandy shores,
So quiet, so quiet, he scarcely snores.

JAMES REEVES

Of Ships
and Men

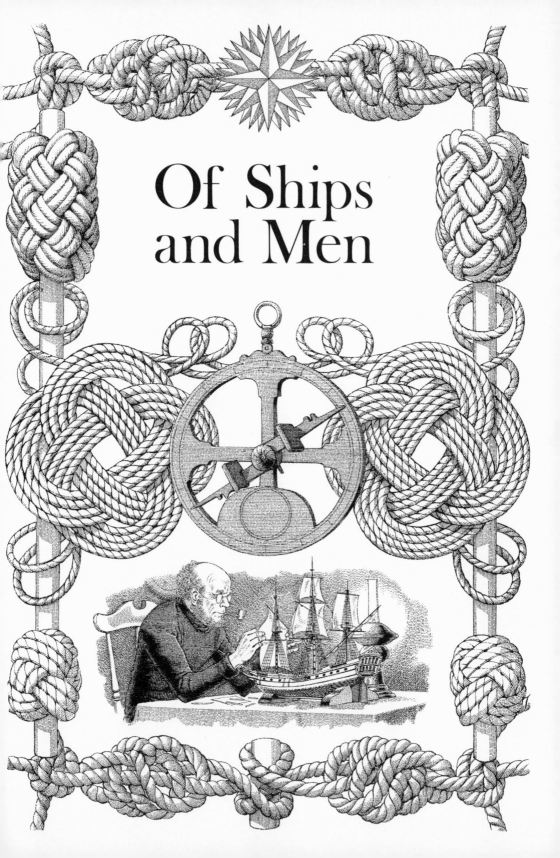

Sea Fever

I must down to the seas again, to the lonely sea and the sky,
And all I ask is a tall ship and a star to steer her by,
And the wheel's kick and the wind's song and the white sail's shaking,
And a gray mist on the sea's face and a gray dawn breaking.

I must down to the seas again, for the call of the running tide
Is a wild call and a clear call that may not be denied;
And all I ask is a windy day with the white clouds flying,
And the flung spray and the blown spume, and the sea gulls crying.

I must down to the seas again, to the vagrant gypsy life,
To the gull's way and the whale's way where the wind's like a whetted knife;
And all I ask is a merry yarn from a laughing fellow-rover,
And quiet sleep and a sweet dream when the long trick's over.

JOHN MASEFIELD

The Sailor's Consolation

One night came on a hurricane,
    The sea was mountains rolling,
When Barney Buntline turned his quid,
    And said to Billy Bowling:
"A strong nor-wester's blowing, Bill;
    Hark! don't ye hear it roar, now?
Lord help 'em, how I pities them
    Unhappy folks on shore now!

"Foolhardy chaps who live in towns,
    What danger they are all in,
And now lie quaking in their beds,
    For fear the roof should fall in;
Poor creatures! how they envies us,
    And wishes, I've a notion,
For our good luck, in such a storm,
    To be upon the ocean!

"And as for them who're out all day
    On business from their houses,
And late at night are coming home,
    To cheer their babes and spouses,
While you and I, Bill, on the deck
    Are comfortably lying,
My eyes! what tiles and chimney pots
    About their heads are flying!

"And very often have we heard
    How men are killed and undone
By overturns of carriages,
    By thieves, and fires in London;
We know what risks all landsmen run,
    From noblemen to tailors;
Then, Bill, let us thank Providence
    That you and I are sailors."

CHARLES DIBDIN

Drake's Drum

Drake he's in his hammock an' a thousand mile away
   (Capten, art tha sleepin' there below?)
Slung atween the round shot in Nombre Dios Bay,
   An' dreamin' arl the time o' Plymouth Hoe.
Yarnder lumes the Island, yarnder lie the ships,
   Wi' sailor lads a-dancin' heel-an'-toe,
An' the shore lights flashin', an' the night tide dashin',
   He sees et arl so plainly as he saw et long ago.

Drake he was a Devon man, an' ruled the Devon seas
   (Capten, art tha sleepin' there below?)
Rovin' tho' his death fell, he went wi' heart at ease,
   An' dreamin' arl the time o' Plymouth Hoe.
"Take my drum to England, hang et by the shore,
   Strike et when your powder's runnin' low;
If the Dons sight Devon, I'll quit the port o' Heaven,
   An' drum them up the Channel as we drumm'd them long ago."

Drake he's in his hammock till the great Armadas come
    (Capten, art tha sleepin' there below?)
Slung atween the round shot, listenin' for the drum,
    An' dreamin' arl the time o' Plymouth Hoe.
Call him on the deep sea, call him up the Sound,
    Call him when ye sail to meet the foe;
Where the old trade's plyin' an' the old flag flyin'
    They shall find him ware an' wakin', as they found him long ago!

SIR HENRY NEWBOLT

Old Ironsides

*Written with Reference to the Proposed Breaking
Up of the Famous U. S. Frigate* Constitution

Ay, tear her tattered ensign down!
    Long has it waved on high,
And many an eye has danced to see
    That banner in the sky;
Beneath it rung the battle shout,
    And burst the cannon's roar:
The meteor of the ocean air
    Shall sweep the clouds no more!

Her deck, once red with heroes' blood,
    Where knelt the vanquished foe,
When winds were hurrying o'er the flood
    And waves were white below,

No more shall feel the victor's tread,
    Or know the conquered knee:
The harpies of the shore shall pluck
    The eagle of the sea!

O better that her shattered hulk
    Should sink beneath the wave!
Her thunders shook the mighty deep,
    And there should be her grave:
Nail to the mast her holy flag,
    Set every threadbare sail,
And give her to the god of storms,
    The lightning and the gale!

OLIVER WENDELL HOLMES

We'll Go to Sea
No More

Oh, blithely shines the bonny sun
    Upon the Isle of May,
And blithely comes the morning tide
    Into St. Andrew's Bay.
Then up, gude-man, the breeze is fair,
    And up, my braw bairns three;
There's gold in yonder bonny boat
    That sails so well the sea.
        When life's last sun goes feebly down,
        And death comes to our door,
        When all the world's a dream to us,
        We'll go to sea no more.

I've seen the waves as blue as air,
    I've seen them green as grass;
But I never feared their heaving yet,
    From Grangemouth to the Bass.
I've seen the sea as black as pitch,
    I've seen it white as snow:
But I never feared its foaming yet,
    Though the winds blew high or low.

When life's last sun goes feebly down,
And death comes to our door,
When all the world's a dream to us,
We'll go to sea no more.

I never liked the landsman's life,
    The earth is aye the same;
Give me the ocean for my dower,
    My vessel for my hame.
Give me the fields that no man ploughs,
    The farm that pays no fee:
Give me the bonny fish that glance
    So gladly through the sea.
        When life's last sun goes feebly down,
        And death comes to our door,
        When all the world's a dream to us,
        We'll go to sea no more.

The sun is up, and round Inchkeith
    The breezes softly blaw;
The gude-man has his lines aboard—
    Awa, my bairns, awa.
An ye'll be back by gloaming gray,
    An bright the fire will low,
An in your tales and songs we'll tell
    How weel the boat ye row.
        When life's last sun goes feebly down,
        And death comes to our door,
        When all the world's a dream to us,
        We'll go to sea no more.

SCOTCH FOLK POEM

Tom Bowling

Here, a sheer hulk, lies poor Tom Bowling,
　　The darling of our crew;
No more he'll hear the tempest howling,
　　For Death has broached him to.
His form was of the manliest beauty,
　　His heart was kind and soft;
Faithful below, he did his duty,
　　But now he's gone aloft.

Tom never from his word departed,
　　His virtues were so rare;
His friends were many and truehearted,
　　His Poll was kind and fair.

And then he'd sing so blithe and jolly;
    Ah, many's the time and oft!
But mirth is turned to melancholy,
    For Tom is gone aloft.

Yet shall poor Tom find pleasant weather,
    When He, who all commands,
Shall give, to call Life's crew together,
    The word to pipe all hands.
Thus Death, who Kings and Tars despatches,
    In vain Tom's life has doffed.
For though his body's under hatches,
    His soul is gone aloft.

CHARLES DIBDIN

Black-eyed Susan

All in the Downs the fleet was moored,
   The streamers waving in the wind,
When black-eyed Susan came aboard;
   "O where shall I my true-love find?
Tell me, ye jovial sailors, tell me true
If my sweet William sails among the crew."

William, who high upon the yard
   Rocked with the billow to and fro,
Soon as her well-known voice he heard
   He sighed, and cast his eyes below:
The cord slides swiftly through his glowing hands,
And quick as lightning on the deck he stands.

So the sweet lark, high poised in air,
    Shuts close his pinions to his breast
If chance his mate's shrill call he hear,
    And drops at once into her nest:
The noblest captain in the British fleet
Might envy William's lip those kisses sweet.

"O Susan, Susan, lovely dear,
    My vows shall ever true remain;
Let me kiss off that falling tear;
    We only part to meet again.
Change as ye list, ye winds; my heart shall be
The faithful compass that still points to thee.

"Believe not what the landmen say
    Who tempt with doubts thy constant mind:
They'll tell thee, sailors, when away,
    In every port a mistress find:
Yes, yes, believe them when they tell thee so,
For Thou art present wheresoe'er I go.

"If to fair India's coast we sail,
    Thy eyes are seen in diamonds bright,
Thy breath is Africa's spicy gale,
    Thy skin is ivory so white.
Thus every beauteous object that I view
Wakes in my soul some charm of lovely Sue.

"Though battle call me from thy arms,
    Let not my pretty Susan mourn;

67

Though cannons roar, yet safe from harms
   William shall to his dear return.
Love turns aside the balls that round me fly,
Lest precious tears should drop from Susan's eye."

The boatswain gave the dreadful word,
   The sails their swelling bosom spread;
No longer must she stay aboard:
   They kissed, she sighed, he hung his head.
Her lessening boat unwilling rows to land;
"Adieu!" she cried; and waved her lily hand.

JOHN GAY

Meditations
of a
Mariner

A-watchin' how the sea behaves
    For hours and hours I sit;
And I know the sea is full o' waves—
    I've often noticed it.

For on the deck each starry night
    The wild waves and the tame
I counts and knows 'em all by sight
    And some of 'em by name.

And then I thinks a cove like me
    Ain't got no right to roam;
For I'm homesick when I puts to sea
    And seasick when I'm home.

WALLACE IRWIN

Wind, Waves, and Sails

Crack of jibing canvas, dazzle-white in the sun,
The harsh cry of a marsh bird,
The flap of pennant in the breeze, or the slop of a halyard
On the mast.
The delicate staccato of wavelets on the waterline.

The shine on steel and sun-shocked
Varnished planking, slippery with moisture.
The scents of summer drifting from the shore.

We move sometimes wafted
By the soft finger-breezes,
Prodding the sail,
Delicate as death
While the world glides softly, swanlike, by.

And sometimes, the gunwale creams the water,
As,
Shell shock, cannon blast,
A squall billows out the shoulder of mutton,
And heels her with a giant sneeze.

Faintly,
From the land, the sound of crickets scraping
Their thin tin whistle piping
In the long straw grasses.

In the reeds
A fish jumps
Snapping greedily at some tasty, winged morsel.
The rudder creaks oil-lessly on its pintles,
The spars groan,
And all is liquid peace.

M. La Rue

Luck

What bring you, sailor, home from the sea—
Coffers of gold and of ivory?

When first I went to sea as a lad
A new jackknife was all I had;

And I've sailed for fifty years and three
To the coasts of gold and of ivory:

And now at the end of a lucky life,
Well, still I've got my old jackknife.

WILFRID GIBSON

Where Lies the Land?

Where lies the land to which the ship would go?
Far, far ahead, is all her seamen know.
And where the land she travels from? Away,
Far, far behind, is all that they can say.

On sunny noons upon the deck's smooth face,
Linked arm and arm, how pleasant here to pace;
Or, o'er the stern reclining, watch below
The foaming wake far-widening as we go.

On stormy nights when wild north-westers rave,
How proud a thing to fight with wind and wave!
The dripping sailor on the reeling mast
Exults to bear, and scorns to wish it past.

Where lies the land to which the ship would go?
Far, far ahead, is all her seamen know.
And where the land she travels from? Away,
Far, far behind, is all that they can say.

ARTHUR HUGH CLOUGH

Cargoes

Quinquireme of Nineveh from distant Ophir,
Rowing home to haven in sunny Palestine,
With a cargo of ivory,
And apes and peacocks,
Sandalwood, cedarwood, and sweet white wine.

Stately Spanish galleon coming from the Isthmus,
Dipping through the Tropics by the palm-green shores,
With a cargo of diamonds,
Emeralds, amethysts,
Topazes, and cinnamon, and gold moidores.

Dirty British coaster with a salt-caked smoke stack,
Butting through the Channel in the mad March days,
With a cargo of Tyne coal,
Road rails, pig lead,
Firewood, ironware, and cheap tin trays.

JOHN MASEFIELD

The Sea Gypsy

I am fevered with the sunset,
I am fretful with the bay,
For the wander-thirst is on me
And my soul is in Cathay.

There's a schooner in the offing,
With her topsails shot with fire,
And my heart has gone aboard her
For the Islands of Desire.

I must forth again tomorrow!
With the sunset I must be
Hull down on the trail of rapture
In the wonder of the sea.

RICHARD HOVEY

The
Sillies

The Powerful Eyes
o' Jeremy Tait

An old seadog on a sailor's log
    Thus spake to a passer-by:
"The most onnatteral thing on earth
    Is the power o' the human eye—
Oh, bless me! yes, oh, blow me! yes—
    It's the power o' the human eye!

"We'd left New York en route for Cork
    A day and a half to sea,
When Jeremy Tait, our fourteenth mate,
    He fastened his eyes on me.

"And wizzle me hook! 'twas a powerful look
    That flashed from them eyes o' his;
I was terrified from heart to hide
    And chilled to me bones and friz.

" 'O Jeremy Tait, O fourteenth mate,'
    I hollers with looks askance,
'Full well I wist ye're a hypnotist,
    So please to remove yer glance!'

"But Jeremy laughed as he turned abaft
    His glance like a demon rat,
And he frightened the cook with his piercin' look,
    And he startled the captain's cat.

"Oh, me, oh, my! When he turned his eye
    On our very efficient crew,
They fell like dead, or they stood like lead
    And stiff as a poker grew.

"So early and late did Jeremy Tait
    That talent o' his employ,
Which caused the crew, and the captain, too,
    Some moments of great annoy.

"For we loved J. Tait, our fourteenth mate,
    As an officer brave and true,
But we quite despised bein' hypnotized
    When we had so much work to do.

"So we grabbed J. Tait, our fourteenth mate
    (His eyes bein' turned away),

By collar and sleeve, and we gave a heave,
  And chucked him into the spray.

"His eyes they flashed as in he splashed,
  But this glance it was sent too late,
For close to our bark a man-eatin' shark
  Jumped after Jeremy Tait.

"And you can bet he would ha' been et
  If he hadn't have did as he done—
Straight at the shark an optical spark
  From his terrible eye he spun.

"Then the shark he shook at Jeremy's look
  And he quailed at Jeremy's glance;
Then he gave a sort of sharkery snort
  And fell right into a trance!

"Quite mesmerized and hypnotized
  That submarine monster lay;
Meek as a shrimp, with his fins all limp,
  He silently floated away.

"So we all of us cried with a conscious pride,
  'Hurrah for Jeremy Tait!'
And we hove a line down into the brine
  And reskied him from his fate.

"And the captain cries, 'We kin use them eyes
  To mighty good purpose soon.
Men, spread the sails—we're a-goin' for whales,
  And we don't need nary harpoon.

" 'For when we hail a blubberous whale
  A-spoutin' the water high,
We'll sail up bold and knock 'im cold
  With the power o' Jeremy's eye!' "

And thus on his log the old sea dog
  Sat whittling nautical chips:
"Oh, powerf'ler far than the human eye
  Is the truth o' the human lips;
But rarest of all is the pearls that fall
  From a truthful mariner's lips."

WALLACE IRWIN

The Alarmed Skipper

Many a long, long year ago,
   Nantucket skippers had a plan
Of finding out, though "lying low,"
   How near New York their schooners ran.

They greased the lead before it fell,
   And then by sounding through the night,
Knowing the soil that stuck so well,
   They always guessed their reckoning right.

A skipper gray, whose eyes were dim,
   Could tell, by tasting, just the spot;
And so below he'd "douse the glim"—
   After, of course, his "something hot."

Snug in his berth at eight o'clock,
   This ancient skipper might be found;
No matter how his craft would rock,
   He slept—for skippers' naps are sound.

The watch on deck would now and then
    Run down and wake him, with the lead;
He'd up and taste, and tell the men
    How many miles they went ahead.

One night 'twas Jotham Marden's watch,
    A curious wag—the peddler's son;
And so he mused (the wanton wretch!),
    "Tonight I'll have a grain of fun.

"We're all a set of stupid fools
    To think the skipper knows, by tasting,
What ground he's on—Nantucket schools
    Don't teach such stuff, with all their basting!"

And so he took a well-greased lead
    And rubbed it o'er a box of earth
That stood on deck—a parsnip-bed—
    And then he sought the skipper's berth.

"Where are we now, sir? Please to taste."
    The skipper yawned, put out his tongue,
Opened his eyes in wondrous haste,
    And then upon the floor he sprung.

The skipper stormed and tore his hair,
    Hauled on his boots, and roared to Marden,
"Nantucket's sunk, and here we are
    Right over old Marm Hackett's garden!"

JAMES T. FIELDS

84

I Saw a Ship

I saw a ship a-sailing,
A-sailing on the sea,
And oh, but it was laden
With pretty things for thee.

There were comfits in the cabin
And apples in the hold;
The sails were made of silk,
And the masts were made of gold.

The four and twenty sailors
That sat upon the deck
Were four and twenty white mice
With chains about their necks.

The captain was a duck
With a packet on his back;
And when the ship began to move,
The captain cried, "Quack! Quack!"

ANONYMOUS

The Uses of Ocean

Lines written in an irresponsible holiday mood

To people who allege that we
Incline to overrate the Sea
    I answer, "We do not;
Apart from being colored blue,
It has its uses not a few;
I cannot think what we should do
    If ever 'the deep did rot.' "

Take ships, for instance. You will note
That, lacking stuff on which to float,
    They could not get about;
Dreadnought and liner, smack and yawl,
And other types that you'll recall—
They simply could not sail at all
    If Ocean once gave out.

And see the trouble which it saves
To islands; but for all those waves
    That made us what we are—
But for their help so kindly lent,
Europe could march right through to Kent
And never need to circumvent
    A single British tar.

Take fish, again. I have in mind
No better field that they could find
    For exercise or sport;
How would the whale, I want to know,
The blubbery whale contrive to blow?
Where would your playful kipper go
    If the supply ran short?

And hence we rank the Ocean high;
But there are privy reasons why
    Its praise is on my lip:
I deem it, when my heart is set
On walking into something wet,
The nicest medium I have met
    In which to take a dip.

OWEN SEAMAN

Captain Pink
of the *Peppermint*

Old Capting Pink of the *Peppermint,*
    Though kindly at heart and good,
Had a blunt, bluff way of a-gittin' 'is say
    That we all of us understood.

When he brained a man with a pingle spike
    Or plastered a seaman flat,
We should 'a' been blowed, but we all of us knowed
    That he didn't mean nothin' by that.

For Capting Pink was a bashful man
    And leary of talk as death,

So he easily saw that a crack in the jaw
　　Was better than wastin' 'is breath.

Sometimes he'd stroll from the ostrich hatch
　　Jest a-feelin' a trifle rum,
Then he'd hang us tars to the masts and spars
　　By a heel or an ear or a thumb.

When he done like that, as he ofttimes did,
　　We winked at each other and smole,
And we snickered in glee and says, says we,
　　"Ain't that like the dear old soul!"

I was wonderful fond of old Capting Pink,
　　And Pink he was fond o' me
(As he frequently said when he battered me head
　　Or sousled me into the sea).

When he sewed the carpenter up in a sack,
　　And fired the cook from a gun,
We'd a-thunk that 'is rule was a little mite crool,
　　If we hadn't knowed Pink as we done.

Old Capting Pink of the *Peppermint,*
　　We all of us loved 'im so
That we waited one night till the tide was right
　　And the funnels was set for a blow.

Then we hauled 'im out of 'is feather bed
　　And hammered the dear old bloke;
And he understood (as we knowed he would)
　　That we done what we did as a joke.

Then we roguishly tumbled 'im over the side,
　　And quickly reversin' the screws,
We hurried away to Mehitabel Bay
　　For a jolly piratical cruise.

Old Capting Pink of the *Peppermint*—
　　I'm shocked and I'm pained to say
That there's few you'll find of the Capting's kind
　　In this here degenerate day.

WALLACE　IRWIN

The Dutiful Mariner

'Twas off the Eastern Filigrees—
   Wizzle the pipes o'ertop!—
When the gallant Captain of the *Cheese*
   Began to skip and hop.

"Oh, stately man and old beside,
   Why dost gymnastics do?
Is such example dignified
   To set before your crew?"

"Oh, hang me crew," the Captain cried,
   "And scuttle of me ship.
If I'm the skipper, blarst me hide!
   Ain't I supposed to skip?

"I'm growing old," the Captain said;
   "Me dancing days are done;
But while I'm skipper of this ship
   I'll skip with any one.

"I'm growing gray," I heard him say,
  "And I cannot rest or sleep
While under me the troubled sea
  Lies forty spasms deep.

"Lies forty spasms deep," he said;
  "But still me trusty sloop
Each hour, I wot, goes many a knot
  And many a bow and loop.

"The hours are full of knots," he said,
  "Untie them if ye can.
In vain I've tried, for Time and Tied
  Wait not for any man.

"Me fate is hard," the old man sobbed,
  "And I am sick and sore.
Me aged limbs of rest are robbed
  And skipping is a bore.

"But Duty is the seaman's boast,
  And on this gallant ship
You'll find the skipper at his post
  As long as he can skip."

And so the Captain of the *Cheese*
  Skipped on again as one
Who lofty satisfaction sees
  In duty bravely done.

WALLACE IRWIN

A Sailor's Yarn

This is the tale that was told to me,
By a battered and shattered son of the sea—
To me and my messmate, Silas Green,
When I was a guileless young marine.

" 'Twas the good ship *Gyascutus,*
    All in the China seas,
With the wind a-lee and the capstan free
    To catch the summer breeze.

" 'Twas Captain Porgie on the deck,
　　To his mate in the mizzen hatch,
While the boatswain bold, in the forward hold,
　　Was winding the larboard watch.

" 'Oh, how does our good ship head tonight?
　　How heads our gallant craft?'
'Oh, she heads to the E.S.W. by N.,
　　And the binnacle lies abaft!'

" 'Oh, what does the quadrant indicate,
　　And how does the sextant stand?'
'Oh, the sextant's down to the freezing point,
　　And the quadrant's lost a hand!'

" 'Oh, and if the quadrant has lost a hand,
　　And the sextant falls so low,
It's our bodies and bones to Davy Jones
　　This night are bound to go!

" 'Oh, fly aloft to the garboard strake!
　　And reef the spanker boom;
Bend a studding sail on the martingale,
　　To give her weather room.

" 'Oh, boatswain, down in the for'ard hold
　　What water do you find?'
'Four foot and a half by the royal gaff
　　And rather more behind!'

" 'Oh, sailors, collar your marline spikes
　　And each belaying pin;

Come stir your stumps, and spike the pumps,
    Or more will be coming in!'

"They stirred their stumps, they spiked the pumps,
    They spliced the mizzen brace;
Aloft and alow they worked, but oh!
    The water gainèd space.

"They bored a hole above the keel
    To let the water out;
But, strange to say, to their dismay,
    The water in did spout.

"Then up spoke the Cook of our gallant ship,
    And he was a lubber brave:
'I have several wives in various ports,
    And my life I'd orter save.'

"Then up spoke the Captain of Marines,
    Who dearly loved his prog:
'It's awful to die, and it's worse to be dry,
    And I move we pipe to grog.'

"Oh, then 'twas the noble second mate
    What filled them all with awe;
The second mate, as bad men hate,
    And cruel skipper's jaw.

"He took the anchor on his back,
    And leaped into the main;
Through foam and spray he clove his way,
    And sunk and rose again!

"Through foam and spray, a league away
    The anchor stout he bore;
Till, safe at last, he made it fast
    And warped the ship ashore!

" 'Taint much of a job to talk about,
    But a ticklish thing to see,
And suth'in to do, if I say it, too,
    For that second mate was me!"

Such was the tale that was told to me
By that modest and truthful son of the sea,
And I envy the life of a second mate,
Though captains curse him and sailors hate,
For he ain't like some of the swabs I've seen,
As would go and lie to a poor marine.

JAMES JEFFREY ROCHE

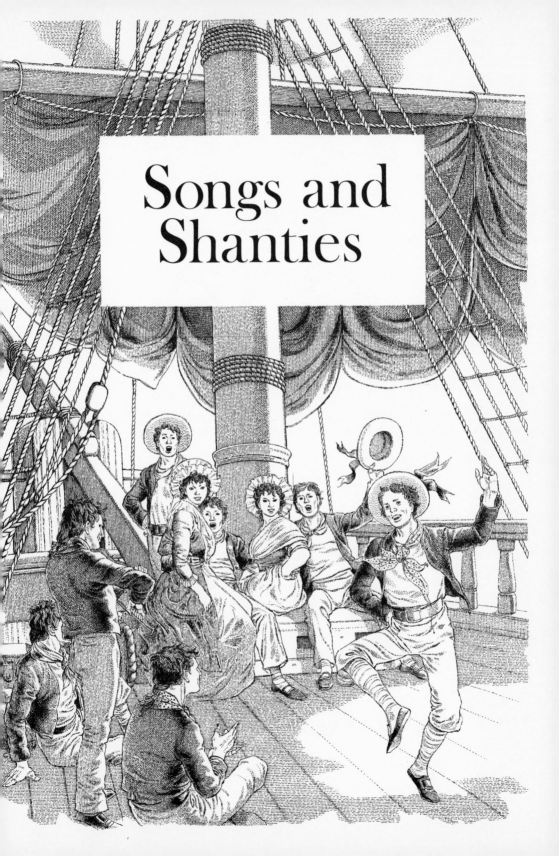

Songs and Shanties

Haul Away Joe

Naow whin Oi wuz a little boy an' so me mother told me,
      'Way haul away, we'll haul away Joe!
That if Oi didn't kiss the gals me lips would all grow mouldy.
      'Way haul away, we'll haul away Joe!

An' Oi sailed the seas for many a year not knowin' what Oi wuz missin',
Then Oi sets me sails afore the gales an' started in a-kissin'.

Naow first Oi got a Spanish gal an' she wuz fat an' lazy,
An' then Oi got a Cuban—she nearly druv me crazy.

Oi courted then a Frenchie gal, she took things free an' aisy,
But naow Oi've got an English gal an' sure she is a daisy.

So list while Oi sing ter yer about me darlin' Nancy,
She's copper-bottomed, clipper-built, she's jist me style an' fancy.

Ye may talk about yer Yankee gals an' round-the-corner Sallies,
But they couldn't make the grade, my bhoys, wid the gals from down our alley.

We sailed away for the China Seas, our bhoys so neat an' handy,
The Ould Man in his cab'n, bhoys, a-drinkin' rum and brandy.

Oh, King Louis wuz the King o' France, afore the Revolution,
But the people cut his big head orf an' spoiled his constitution.

Saint Patrick wuz a gintleman, an' he come of daycent paypul,
He built a church in Dublin town an' on it set a staypul.

From Oireland thin he druv the snakes, then drank up all the whisky,
   'Way haul away, we'll haul away Joe!
This made him dance an' sing an' jig, he felt so fine an' frisky.
   'Way haul away, we'll haul away Joe!

SEA SHANTY (IRISH VERSION)

100

Come Loose Every Sail
to the Breeze

Come loose ev'ry sail to the breeze,
The course of my vessel improve;
I've done with the toils of the seas,
Ye sailors, I'm bound to my love.

> *Ye sailors, I'm bound to my love,*
> *Ye sailors, I'm bound to my love,*
> *I've done with the toils of the seas,*
> *Ye sailors, I'm bound to my love.*

Since Emma is true as she's fair,
My griefs I fling all to the wind;
'Tis a pleasing return for my care,
My mistress is constant and kind.

101

My sails are all filled to my dear,
What tropic bird swifter can move?
Who, cruel, shall hold his career,
That returns to the nest of his love?

Then hoist every sail to the breeze,
Come, shipmates, and join in the song;
Let's drink while the ship cuts the seas,
To the gale that may drive her along.

Ye sailors, I'm bound to my love,
Ye sailors, I'm bound to my love,
I've done with the toils of the seas,
Ye sailors, I'm bound to my love.

SEA SHANTY

The Eddystone Light

Me father was the keeper of the Eddystone Light,
He married a mer-my-aid one night;
Out of the match came children three—
Two was fish and the other was me.

> *Jolly stories, jolly told*
> *When the winds is bleak and the nights is cold;*
> *No such life can be led on the shore*
> *As is had on the rocks by the ocean's roar.*

When I was but a boyish chip,
They put me in charge of the old lightship;
I trimmed the lamps and I filled 'em with oil,
And I played Seven-up accordin' to Hoyle.

One evenin' as I was a-trimmin' the glim
An' singin' a verse of the evenin' hymn,
I see by the light of me binnacle lamp
Me kind old father lookin' jolly and damp;
An' a voice from the starboard shouted "Ahoy!"
An' there was me gran'mother sittin' on a buoy—
Meanin' a buoy for ships what sail
An' not a boy what's a juvenile male.

> *Jolly stories, jolly told*
> *When the winds is bleak and the nights is cold;*
> *No such life can be led on the shore*
> *As is had on the rocks by the ocean's roar.*

ENGLISH FOLK SONG

Blow, Ye Winds

'Twas on a Sunday mornin', down 'cross the Southern Sea,
Our ship she lay at anchor, while a-waitin' for a breeze.
> *Singin', blow, ye winds, in the mornin',*
> *Blow, ye winds, high-ho!*
> *Clear away yer runnin' gear*
> *An' blow, me bully boys, blow!*

The cap'n he wuz down below, the men at their work about,
When under our bow we heard a splash, an' then a lusty shout.

"Man overboard!" the lookout cried, an' for'ard we all ran,
An' hangin' to the larbord chains wuz a bluff ol' green merman.

His hair wuz blue, his eyes wuz green, his mouth wuz big as three,
An' the long green tail that he sat on wuz wigglin' in the sea.

"Hello!" cried the Mate as bold as brass, "What-ho! shipmates," cried he.
"Oh, I want ter speak ter yer Ol' Man, I've a favor to ask, ye see.

"I've bin out all night on a ruddy sea fight at the bottom of the deep blue sea;
I've just come home and find that ye have caused a hell o' a spree.

"Oh, ye've dropped yer anchor afore me house, an' blocked me only door,
An' me wife's blocked in an' she can't git out, nor me babes who number four."

"The anchor shall be hove at once, an' yer wife an' yer babes set free,
But I never saw a scale from a sprat to a whale till now that could speak to me.

"Yer figgerhead is a sailor's bold, an' ye speak like a human man,
But where did yer git such a ruddy big tail? Answer me that if yer can."

"A long time ago from the ship *Hero* I fell overboard in a gale,
An' away down below where the seaweeds grow, I met a gal with a tail.

"She saved me life, an' I made her me wife, an' me legs changed instantly,
An' now I'm married to a sweet mermaid at the bottom of the deep blue sea.

"So I'll stay here for the rest o 'me life, with never a worry nor care.
Good-by to the trade of a sailor bold—my lot with the fishes I'll share."

> *Singin', blow, ye winds, in the mornin',*
> *Blow, ye winds, high-ho!*
> *Clear away yer runnin' gear*
> *An' blow, me bully boys, blow!*

ENGLISH SEA SHANTY

106

The Fishes

Oh, a ship she was rigg'd, and ready for sea,
And all of her sailors were fishes to be.

> *Windy weather! Stormy weather!*
> *When the wind blows we're all together.*
> *Blow, ye winds, westerly, gentle southwesterly,*
> *Blow, ye winds, westerly—steady she goes.*

Oh, the first came the herring, the king of the sea,
He jumped on the poop, "I'll be captain," said he.

The next was a flatfish, they call him the skate,
"If you be the captain, why, sure, I'm the mate."

The next came the hake, as black as a rook,
Says he, "I'm no sailor, I'll ship as the cook."

The next came the shark, with his two rows of teeth:
"Cook, mind the cabbage, and I'll mind the beef."

And then came the codfish, with his chucklehead,
He jumped in the chains, began heaving the lead.

The next came the flounder, as flat as the ground:
"Chucklehead, damn your eyes, mind how you sound."

The next comes the mack'rel, with his stripèd back,
He jumped to the waist for to board the main tack.

And then came the sprat, the smallest of all,
He jumped on the poop, and cried, "Main-topsail haul."

Windy weather! Stormy weather!
When the wind blows we're all together.
Blow, ye winds, westerly, gentle southwesterly,
Blow, ye winds, westerly—steady she goes.

SEA SHANTY

The Mermaid

'Twas Friday morn when we set sail,
   And we were not far from the land,
When the captain he spied a pretty mermaid
   With a comb and a glass in her hand.

    Oh, the ocean waves do roll,
    And the stormy winds do blow,
    While we poor sailors go skipping to the top
    And the landlubbers lie down below.

Then up spoke the captain of our gallant ship,
   And a well-spoken man was he,
"Oh, I have a wife in Salem town,
   And tonight a widow she'll be."

Then up spoke the cook of our gallant ship,
    And a crazy old butcher was he,
"I care far more for me kettles and me pans
    Than I do for the bottom of the sea."

Then up spoke the cabin boy of our gallant ship,
    And a brave young lad was he,
"Oh, I have a sweetheart in Salem by the sea,
    And tonight she'll be weeping for me."

Then three times 'round spun our gallant ship,
    And three times 'round spun she,
And three times 'round spun our gallant ship,
    And she sank to the bottom of the sea.

    Oh, the ocean waves do roll,
    And the stormy winds do blow,
    While we poor sailors go skipping to the top
    And the landlubbers lie down below.

ENGLISH SONG

The Gals o' Dublin Town

Sometimes we're bound for Liverpool, sometimes we're bound for France,
But now we're bound to Dublin town to give the gals a chance.

> *Hurrah! Hurrah! for the gals o' Dub-a-lin town,*
> *Hurrah for the bonnie green flag an' the Harp without the Crown!*

Sometimes we're bound for furrin parts, sometimes we're bound for home,
A Johnny's always at his best wherever he may roam.

Sometimes the weather's fine an' fair, sometimes it's darn well foul,
Sometimes it blows a Cape 'Orn gale that freezes up yer soul.

Sometimes we works as hard as hell, sometimes our grub it stinks,
Enough to make a sojer curse, or make a bishop blink.

Sometimes we wisht we'd niver jined, sometimes we'd like to be
A-drinkin' in a pub, me bhoys, a gal sat on each knee.

Sometimes we are a happy crowd, sometimes we'll sing a song,
Sometimes we wish we'd niver bin born, but we do not grouse for long.

An' when the voyage is all done, an' we go away on shore,
We'll spend our money on the gals, 'n' go to sea for more!

    Hurrah! Hurrah! for the gals o' Dub-a-lin town,
    Hurrah for the bonnie green flag an' the Harp without the Crown!

IRISH SEA SHANTY

The Chinee Bumboatman

I'll sing ye a story o' trouble an' woe that'll cause ye to shudder an' shiver,
Concarnin' a Chinee bumboatman that sailed the Yang-Tze River.
He was a heathen o' 'igh degree, as the joss-house records show,
His family name wuz Wing Chang Loo, but the sailors all called him Jim
　　Crow-ee-eye-oh-ee-eye!

　　Hitchee-kum, kitchee-kum, ya! ya! ya!
　　Sailorman no likee me,
　　No savvy the story of Wing Chang Loo,
　　Too much of the bober-eye-ee, kye-eye!

Now Wing Chang Loo he fell in love with a gal called Ah Chu Fong;
She 'ad two eyes like pumpkin seeds, an' slippers two inches long.
But Ah Chu Fong loved a pirate bold with all her heart and liver;
He wuz captain of a double-decked junk, an' he sailed the Yang-Tze River-eye-
iver-eye!

When Wing Chang Loo he heard o' this, he swore an 'orrible oath:
"If Ah Chu marries that pirate bold, I'll make sausage meat o' 'em both."
So he hoisted his blood-red battle flag, put into the Yang-Tze River;
He steered her east an' south an' west, till that pirate he did diskiver-eye-iver-eye.

The drums they beat to quarters an' the cannons did loudly roar,
The red-'ot dumplin's flew like lead, an' the scuppers they ran with gore;
The pirate paced the quarter-deck with never a shake nor a shiver,
He wuz shot in the stern wi' a hard-boiled egg that pinitrated his liver-eye-iver-eye.

The dyin' pirate feebly cried, "We'll give the foe more shot;
If I can't marry Ah Chu Fong, then Wing Chang Loo shall not."
When a pease-pudden 'ot hit the bumboat's side, it caused a 'orrible scene,
It upset a pot of 'ot bow-wow soup, an' exploded the Magazye-eenee-aye-eenee!

ENGLISH SEA SHANTY

The Whale

'Twas in the year of forty-nine,
   On March, the twentieth day,
Our gallant ship her anchor weigh'd,
   And to the sea she bore away,
      Brave boys,
   And to the sea she bore away.

Old Blowhard was our captain's name,
   Our ship the *Lion* bold,
And we were bound to the North Country
   To face the frost and the cold.

And when we came to that cold country
   Where the ice and the snow do lie,
Where there's ice and snow, and the great whales blow,
   And the daylight does not die,

Our mate went up to the topmast head
   With a spyglass in his hand:

"A whale, a whale, a whale," he cries,
  "And she spouts at every span."

Up jumped old Blowhard on the deck—
  And a clever little man was he—
"Overhaul, overhaul, let your main-tackle fall,
  And launch your boat to sea."

We struck that fish and away she flew
  With a flourish of her tail;
But oh! and alas! we lost one man
  And we did not catch that whale.

Now when the news to our captain came
  He called up all his crew,
And for the losing of that man
  He down his colors drew.

Says he: "My men, be not dismayed
  At the losing of one man,
For Providence will have his will,
  Let man do what he can."

Now the losing of that prentice boy
  It grieved our captain sore,
But the losing of that great big whale
  It grieved him a damned sight more,
    Brave boys,
  It grieved him a damned sight more.

AMERICAN SEA SHANTY

A Long Time Ago

Three ships they lay in Frisco Bay,
Three ships they lay in Frisco Bay.

An' one o' these packets wuz ol' Noah's Ark,
All covered all over with hickory bark.

They filled up her seams with oakum an' pitch,
Her sails wuz badly in need o' a stitch.

Her bow it wuz bluff an' her counter wuz round,
Her knees wuz so thin, an' her timbers unsound.

Her fo'c's'le wuz low, an' her starn wuz too high,
The hold for the animals never wuz dry.

Her pumps they wuz jammed and her fores'l wuz torn,
She looked like an ol' Spanish galley-eye-orn.

Now this is the gangway the animals went down,
An' this is the hold where they walk round an' round.

Ol' Noah of old he commanded this Ark,
His cargo wuz animals out for a lark.

He boarded the animals, two of each kind,
Birds, snakes, an' jiggy-bugs, he didn't mind.

The animals rolled up, oh, two by two
The elephant chasin' the kangaroo.

The bull an' the cow they started a row,
The bull did his best to horn the cow.

Then Ol' Noah said with a flick o' his whip,
"Stop this bloody row, or I'll scuttle the ship."

An' the bull put his horns through the side o' the Ark,
An' the little black doggie, he started to bark.

So Noah took the dog, put his nose in the hole,
An' ever since then the dog's nose has been cold.

The animals came in three by three,
The elephant ridin' the back o' the flea.

The animals came in four by four,
Ol' Noah went mad an' he hollered for more.

The animals came in five by five,
Some wuz half dead, an' some half alive.

The animals came in six by six,
The hyena laughed at the monkey's tricks.

The monkey was dressed up in soger's clo'es;
Where he got 'em from, God only knows.

The animals came in seven by seven,
Sez the ant to the elephant, "Who are yer shovin'?"

The animals came in eight by eight,
A drunken big chimp an' a scabby big ape.

The animals came in nine by nine,
The sea lions havin' a bloomin' fine time.

The animals came in ten by ten,
The Ark with a shriek blew her whistle then.

An' Noah while working at loading her stock,
Had anchored the Ark with a bloody great rock.

Ol' Noah he then hove the gangplank in,
An' then the long voyage it sure did begin.

They hadn't the foggiest where they wuz at,
Until they piled right up on ol' Ararat.

The ol' Ark with a bump landed high an' dry,
And the bear give the turkey a sailor's good-by.

I thought that I heard Ol' Noah say,
"Give one more pull lads, an' then belay!"

AMERICAN SEA SHANTY

The *Irish Rover*

In the year of our Lord eighteen hundred and six,
    We set sail from the fair Cove of Cork.
We were bound far away with a cargo of bricks
    For the grand City Hall in New York.
We'd an elegant craft, she was rigged fore and aft,
    Oh, how the trade winds drove her;
She had twenty-three masts, and she stood fearful blasts,
    And they called her the *Irish Rover*.

There was Barney Magee from the banks of the Lee,
    O'Neill and McClain from the Rhine;
There was Johnny McGurk, who was scared stiff of work,
    Mike McClone, Pat Malone, and O'Brien.
There was Slugger O'Toole, who was drunk as a rule,
    And Michael O'Dowd from Dover;
And a man from Turkestan, his name was Tim McCann,
    Was the skipper of the *Irish Rover*.

We had one million bags of the best Sligo rags,
  We had two million barrels of bone;
We had three million bales of old nanny goat's tails,
  We had four million barrels of stone.
We had five million cats and six million rats,
  And seven million barrels of porter;
We had eight million sides of old blind horse's hides,
  In the hold of the *Irish Rover*.

We had sailed seven years when the measles broke out,
  And our ship lost her way in the fog;
And the whole of the crew was reduced down to two,
  'Twas myself and the captain's old dog.
Then she struck on a rock with a terrible shock,
  And oh, she keeled right over,
Turned nine times around, and the old dog was drowned;
  I'm the last of the *Irish Rover*.

IRISH SONG

Sea Chanty

Salt Water Type Song

Our ship is leaving Portsmouth town,
Her name's the good ship *Nancy Brown*.
    Yo ho,
    Jib the boom,
    Poop the deck,
    Rattle the hatch,
    Main the sail,
    Pepper the mints,
    Anchors aweigh in the morn.

Oh, we'll be sailing with the tide,
We've said farewell to our girls and brides,
    Yo ho,
    Rig the ratch,
    Hoist the hitch,
    Bury the hatchet,
    Poop the deck,
    Beat the breeze,
    That she blows in the morn.

And soon we'll be out on the ocean foam,
So let's heave ho with a will,
And come, jolly tars, let's sing while we can,
For soon we'll all be deathly ill!

For there's nothing like the life of a sailor,
Sailing on the briny foam,
With a good stout ship beneath your feet,
And a good stout wife at home.

Oh, there's nothing, nothing, nothing like the sailor's life,
The sailor's life is grand,
Oh, I'd never give up the sea unless
You offered me a job on land.

So it's three jolly cheers for the sea,
And a fond farewell to dry land,
So up with the anchor and we won't set it down
Till we reach old Coney Island!

Singing yo ho,
Hit the deck,
Follow the fleet,
Anchor's aweigh,
Scuttle the butt,
Roll the dice,
Deal the cards,
Pepper the mints,
We're sailing away on the sea.

ABE BURROWS

123

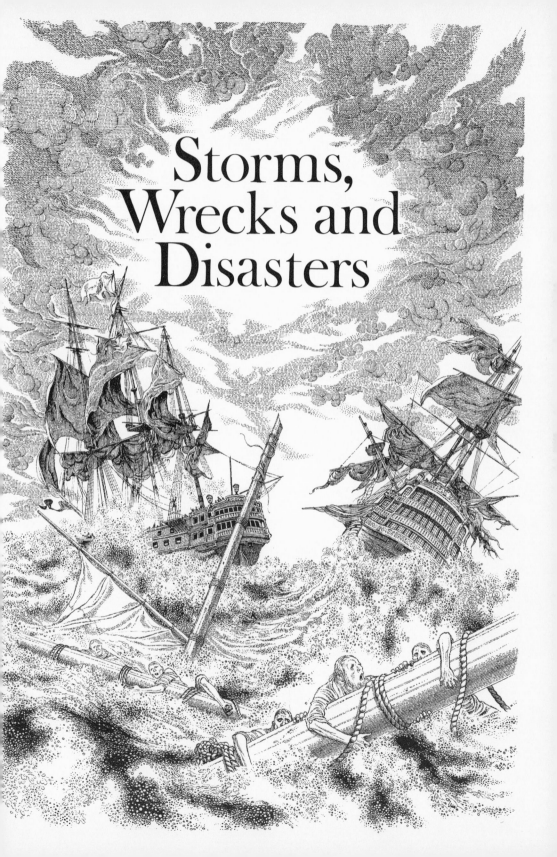

Storms, Wrecks and Disasters

The Wreckers' Prayer

(*Newfoundland*)

Give us a wrack or two, Good Lard,
For winter in Tops'il Tickle bes hard,
Wid gray frost creepin' like mortal sin
And perishin' lack of bread in the bin.

A grand rich wrack, us do humbly pray,
Busted abroad at the break o' day
An' hove clear in 'crost Tops'il Reef,
Wid victuals an' gear to beguile our grief.

God of reefs an' tides an' sky,
Heed ye our need and hark to our cry!
Bread by the bag an' beef by the cask—
Ease for sore bellies bes all we ask.

One grand wrack—or maybe two?—
Wid gear an' victuals to see us through
'Til Spring starts up like the leap of day
An' the fish strike back into Tops'il Bay.

One rich wrack—for Thy hand bes strong!
A barque or a brig from up-along
Bemused by the twisty tides, O Lard!
For winter in Tops'il Tickle bes hard.

Loud an' long will us sing yer praise,
Merciful Fadder, O Ancient of Days,
Master of fog, an' tide, an' reef!
Heave us a wrack to beguile our grief. Amen.

THEODORE GOODRIDGE ROBERTS

Sir Patrick Spence

The king sits in Dumferling toune,
    Drinking the blude-reid wine:
"O whar will I get a guid sailor,
    To sail this schip of mine?"

Up and spak an eldlern knicht,
    Sat at the king's richt kne;
"Sir Patrick Spence is the best sailor
    That sails upon the se."

The king has written a braid letter,
    And signed it wi' his hand,
And sent it to Sir Patrick Spence,
    Was walking on the sand.

The first line that Sir Patrick red,
    A loud lauch lauched he;
The next line that Sir Patrick red,
    The teir blinded his ee.

"O wha is this has done this deid,
    This ill deid don to me,
To send me out this time o' the yeir,
    To sail upon the se!

---

braid: strong

"Mak haste, mak haste, my mirry men all,
   Our guid schip sails the morne":
"O say na sae, my master deir,
   Fir I feir a deadlie storme.

"Late, late yestreen I saw the new moone,
   Wi' the auld moone in hir arme,
And I feir, I feir, my deir master,
   That we will cum to harme."

O our Scots nobles wer richt laith
   To weet their cork-heil'd schoone;
Bot lang owre a' the play wer playd,
   Thair hats they swam aboone.

O lang, lang may their ladies sit
   Wi' thair fans into their hand,
Or eir they se Sir Patrick Spence
   Cum sailing to the land.

O lang, lang may the ladies stand,
   Wi' thair gold kems in their hair,
Waiting for thair ain deir lords,
   For they'll se thame na mair.

Haf owre, haf owre to Aberdour,
   It's fiftie fadom deip,
And thair lies guid Sir Patrick Spence,
   Wi' the Scots lords at his feit.

SCOTCH BALLAD

---

richt laith: right loath   *weet:* wet   *Bot lang owre:* But long before

from The Rhyme
of the Ancient Mariner

And now the storm blast came, and he
    Was tyrannous and strong;
He struck with his o'ertaking wings,
    And chas'd us south along.

With sloping masts and dripping prow,
As who pursued with yell and blow
Still treads the shadow of his foe,
    And forward bends his head,
The ship drove fast, loud roared the blast,
    And southward aye we fled.

And now there came both mist and snow,
    And it grew wondrous cold;
And ice, mast-high, came floating by,
    As green as emerald.

And through the drifts the snowy clifts
    Did send a dismal sheen;

Nor shapes of men nor beasts we ken—
    The ice was all between.

The ice was here, the ice was there,
    The ice was all around;
It cracked and growled, and roared and howled,
    Like noises in a swound.

At length did cross an Albatross,
    Through the fog it came;
As if it had been a Christian soul,
    We hailed it in God's name.

It ate the food it ne'er had eat,
    And round and round it flew,
The ice did split with a thunder-fit;
    The helmsman steered us through!

SAMUEL TAYLOR COLERIDGE

The Albatross

I sailed below the Southern Cross
    (So ran the seaman's song);
A pestilential albatross
    Followed us all day long.

The creature's aspect was so grim,
    And it oppressed me so,
I raised . . . then, on a sudden whim,
    I lowered my crossbow.

The weather grew exceeding thick;
    The sullen tempest roared.
A dozen of the crew fell sick,
    The rest fell overboard.

The skies were so devoid of light
   We could not see to pray.
The donkeyman went mad by night,
   The second mate by day.

We set the live men swabbing decks,
   The dead man manned the pumps.
The cabin steward changed his sex;
   The captain had the mumps.

The cargo shifted in the hold,
   The galley boiler burst.
My hair turned white, my blood ran cold—
   I knew we were accurst.

I helped the purser dig his grave
   On the deserted poop;
I leaped into the foaming wave
   And swam to Guadeloupe.

And there (he said) I nibbled moss
   Beside the stagnant lake . . .
I should have shot the albatross,
   That was my big mistake.

R. P. LISTER

The *Titanic*

Oh, they built the ship *Titanic*, and they built her strong and true,
And they built her so that the water would not come through,
But the Lord's almighty hand knew that ship would never land—
It was sad when that great ship went down.

> *It was sad, it was sad,*
> *It was sad when the great ship went down;*
> *Husbands and wives, little children lost their lives,*
> *It was sad when the great ship went down.*

Oh, they sailed from England, and were almost to the shore
When the rich refused to associate with the poor,
So they put 'em down below, where they'd be the first to go—
It was sad when that great ship went down.

135

The boat was full of sin, and the sides about to burst,
When the captain shouted, "A-women and children first!"
Oh, the captain tried to wire, but the lines were all on fire—
It was sad when that great ship went down.

Oh, they swung the lifeboats out o'er the deep and raging sea,
When the band struck up with "A-nearer My God to Thee";
Little children wept and cried as the waves swept o'er the side—
It was sad when that great ship went down.

It was sad, it was sad,
It was sad when the great ship went down;
Husbands and wives, little children lost their lives,
It was sad when the great ship went down.

AMERICAN FOLK SONG

Loss of
the *Royal George*

Toll for the brave—
The brave that are no more!
All sunk beneath the wave
Fast by their native shore!

Eight hundred of the brave,
Whose courage well was tried,
Had made the vessel heel
And laid her on her side.

A land breeze shook the shrouds
And she was overset;
Down went the *Royal George,*
With all her crew complete.

Toll for the brave!
Brave Kempenfelt is gone;
His last sea fight is fought,
His work of glory done.

It was not in the battle;
No tempest gave the shock;
She sprang no fatal leak,
She ran upon no rock.

His sword was in its sheath,
His fingers held the pen,
When Kempenfelt went down
With twice four hundred men.

—Weigh the vessel up
Once dreaded by our foes!
And mingle with our cup
The tears that England owes.

Her timbers yet are sound,
And she may float again
Full charged with England's thunder,
And plow the distant main;

But Kempenfelt is gone,
His victories are o'er;
And he and his eight hundred
Shall plow the wave no more.

WILLIAM COWPER

The Yarn of
the *Loch Achray*

The *Loch Achray* was a clipper tall
With seven and twenty hands in all.
Twenty to hand and reef and haul,
A skipper to sail and mates to bawl,
"Tally on to the tackle fall,
Heave now 'n' start her, heave 'n' pawl!"
    Hear the yarn of a sailor,
    An old yarn learned at sea.

Her crew were shipped and they said, "Farewell,
So long, my Tottie, my lovely gell;
We sail today if we fetch to hell,
It's time we tackled the wheel a spell."
    Hear the yarn of a sailor,
    An old yarn learned at sea.

The dockside loafers talked on the quay
The day that she towed down to sea:
"Lord, what a handsome ship she be!

Cheer her, sonny boys, three times three!"
And the dockside loafers gave her a shout
As the red-funnelled tugboat towed her out;
They gave her a cheer as the custom is,
And the crew yelled, "Take our loves to Liz—
Three cheers, bullies, for old Pier Head
'N' the bloody stay-at-homes!" they said.
     Hear the yarn of a sailor,
     An old yarn learned at sea.

In the gray of the coming on of night
She dropped the tug at the Tuskar Light,
'N' the topsails went to the topmast head
To a chorus that fairly awoke the dead.
She trimmed her yards and slanted South
With her royals set and a bone in her mouth.
     Hear the yarn of a sailor,
     An old yarn learned at sea.

She crossed the Line and all went well,
They ate, they slept, and they struck the bell,
And I give you a gospel truth when I state
The crowd didn't find any fault with the Mate,
But one night off of the River Plate.
     Hear the yarn of a sailor,
     An old yarn learned at sea.

It freshened up till it blew like thunder
And burrowed her deep lee-scuppers under.
The old man said, "I mean to hang on
Till her canvas busts or her sticks are gone"—

Which the blushing looney did, till at last
Overboard went her mizzenmast.
     Hear the yarn of a sailor,
     An old yarn learned at sea.

Then a fierce squall struck the *Loch Achray*
And bowed her down to her waterway;
Her main-shrouds gave and her forestay,
And a green sea carried her wheel away;
Ere the watch below had time to dress
She was cluttered up in a blushing mess.
     Hear the yarn of a sailor,
     An old yarn learned at sea.

She couldn't lay-to nor yet pay-off,
And she got swept clean in the bloody trough;
Her masts were gone, and afore you knowed
She filled by the head and down she goed.
Her crew made seven-and-twenty dishes
For the big jack-sharks and the little fishes,
And over their bones the water swishes.
     Hear the yarn of a sailor,
     An old yarn learned at sea.

The wives and girls they watch in the rain
For a ship as won't come home again.
"I reckon it's them head winds," they say,
"She'll be home tomorrow, if not today.
I'll just nip home 'n' I'll air the sheets
'N' buy the fixins 'n' cook the meats
As my man likes 'n' as my man eats."

So home they goes by the windy streets,
Thinking their men are homeward bound
With anchors hungry for English ground,
And the bloody fun of it is, they're drowned!
Hear the yarn of a sailor,
An old yarn learned at sea.

JOHN MASEFIELD

Robinson Crusoe's Story

The night was thick and hazy
When the *Piccadilly Daisy*
Carried down the crew and captain in the sea;
And I think the water drowned 'em,
For they never, never found 'em,
And I know they didn't come ashore with me.

Oh! 'twas very sad and lonely
When I found myself the only
Population on this cultivated shore;
But I've made a little tavern
In a rocky little cavern,
And I sit and watch for people at the door.

I spent no time in looking
  For a girl to do my cooking,
As I'm quite a clever hand at making stews;
  But I had that fellow Friday
  Just to keep the tavern tidy,
And to put a Sunday polish on my shoes.

I have a little garden
  That I'm cultivating lard in,
As the things I eat are rather tough and dry;
  For I live on toasted lizards,
  Prickly pears and parrot gizzards,
And I'm really very fond of beetle pie.

The clothes I had were furry,
  And it made me fret and worry
When I found the moths were eating off the hair;
  And I had to scrape and sand 'em,
  And I boiled 'em and I tanned 'em,
Till I got the fine morocco suit I wear.

I sometimes seek diversion
  In a family excursion,
With the few domestic animals you see;
  And we take along a carrot
  As refreshment for the parrot,
And a little can of jungle-berry tea.

Then we gather as we travel
  Bits of moss and dirty gravel,
And we chip off little specimens of stone;

And we carry home as prizes
Funny bugs of handy sizes,
Just to give the day a scientific tone.

If the roads are wet and muddy
We remain at home and study—
For the Goat is very clever at a sum,
And the Dog, instead of fighting,
Studies ornamental writing,
While the Cat is taking lessons on the drum.

We retire at eleven,
And we rise again at seven;
And I wish to call attention, as I close,
To the fact that all the scholars
Are correct about their collars,
And particular in turning out their toes.

CHARLES EDWARD CARRYL

The Circus Ship *Euzkera*

Lost in the Caribbean Sea, September 1948

The most stupendous show they ever gave
Must have been that *bizarrerie* of wreck;
The lion tamer spoke from a green wave
And lions slithered slowly off the deck.

Amazing! And the high-wire artists fell
(As we'd all hoped, in secret) through no net
And ten miles down, a plunge they must know well,
And landed soft, and there they're lying yet.

Then while the brass band played a languid waltz,
The elephant, in pearls and amethysts,
Toppled and turned his ponderous somersaults,
Dismaying some remote geologists.

The tiger followed, and the tiger's mate.
The seals leaped joyful from their brackish tank.
The fortuneteller read the palm of Fate—
Beware of ocean voyages—and sank.

Full fathom five the fattest lady lies,
Among the popcorn and the caged baboons,
And dreams of mermaids' elegant surprise
To see the bunting and the blue balloons.

WALKER GIBSON

146

Skipper Ireson's Ride

Of all the rides since the birth of time,
Told in story or sung in rhyme—
On Apuleius's Golden Ass,
Or one-eyed Calender's horse of brass,
Witch astride of a human back,
Islam's prophet on Al-Borák—
The strangest ride that ever was sped
Was Ireson's, out from Marblehead!
   Old Floyd Ireson, for his hard heart,
    Tarred and feathered and carried in a cart
      By the women of Marblehead!

Body of turkey, head of owl,
Wings a-droop like a rained-on fowl,
Feathered and ruffled in every part,
Skipper Ireson stood in the cart.

Scores of women, old and young,
Strong of muscle, and glib of tongue,
Pushed and pulled up the rocky lane,
Shouting and singing the shrill refrain:
   "Here's Flud Oirson, fur his horrd horrt,
   Torr'd an' futherr'd an' corr'd in a corrt
     By the women o' Morble'ead!"

Wrinkled scolds with hands on hips,
Girls in bloom of cheek and lips,
Wild-eyed, free-limbed, such as chase
Bacchus round some antique vase,
Brief of skirt, with ankles bare,
Loose of kerchief and loose of hair,
With conch shells blowing and fish horns' twang,
Over and over the Maenads sang:
   "Here's Flud Oirson, fur his horrd horrt,
   Torr'd an' futherr'd an' corr'd in a corrt
     By the women o' Morble'ead!"

Small pity for him!—He sailed away
From a leaking ship in Chaleur Bay—
Sailed away from a sinking wreck,
With his own townspeople on her deck!
"Lay by! lay by!" they called to him.
Back he answered, "Sink or swim!
Brag of your catch of fish again!"
And off he sailed through the fog and rain!
   Old Floyd Ireson, for his hard heart,
   Tarred and feathered and carried in a cart
     By the women of Marblehead!

Fathoms deep in dark Chaleur
That wreck shall lie forevermore.
Mother and sister, wife and maid,
Looked from the rocks of Marblehead
Over the moaning and rainy sea—
Looked for the coming that might not be!
What did the winds and the sea birds say
Of the cruel captain who sailed away?
   Old Floyd Ireson, for his hard heart,
    Tarred and feathered and carried in a cart
     By the women of Marblehead!

Through the street, on either side,
Up flew windows, doors swung wide;
Sharp-tongued spinsters, old wives gray,
Treble lent the fish horn's bray.
Sea-worn grandsires, cripple-bound,
Hulks of old sailors run aground,
Shook head, and fist, and hat, and cane,
And cracked with curses the hoarse refrain:
   "Here's Flud Oirson, fur his horrd horrt,
    Torr'd an' futherr'd an' corr'd in a corrt
     By the women o' Morble'ead!"

Sweetly along the Salem road
Bloom of orchard and lilac showed.
Little the wicked skipper knew
Of the fields so green and the sky so blue.
Riding there in his sorry trim,
Like an Indian idol glum and grim,
Scarcely he seemed the sound to hear

Of voices shouting, far and near:
    "Here's Flud Oirson, fur his horrd horrt,
    Torr'd an' futherr'd an' corr'd in a corrt
      By the women o' Morble'ead!"

"Hear me, neighbors!" at last he cried—
"What to me is this noisy ride?
What is the shame that clothes the skin
To the nameless horror that lives within?
Waking or sleeping, I see a wreck,
And hear a cry from a reeling deck!
Hate me and curse me—I only dread
The hand of God and the face of the dead!"
    Said old Floyd Ireson, for his hard heart,
    Tarred and feathered and carried in a cart
      By the women of Marblehead!

Then the wife of the skipper lost at sea
Said, "God has touched him! why should we!"
Said an old wife mourning her only son,
"Cut the rogue's tether and let him run!"
So with soft relentings and rude excuse,
Half scorn, half pity, they cut him loose,
And gave him a cloak to hide him in,
And left him alone with his shame and sin.
    Poor Floyd Ireson, for his hard heart,
    Tarred and feathered and carried in a cart
      By the women of Marblehead!

JOHN GREENLEAF WHITTIER

Brave Alum Bey

Oh, big was the bosom of brave ALUM BEY,
And also the region that under it lay,
In safety and peril remarkably cool,
And he dwelt on the banks of the river Stamboul.

Each morning he went to his garden, to cull
A bunch of zenana or sprig of bul-bul,
And offered the bouquet, in exquisite bloom,
To BACKSHEESH, the daughter of RAHAT LAKOUM.

No maiden like BACKSHEESH could tastily cook
A kettle of kismet or joint of tchibouk,
As ALUM, brave fellow! sat pensively by,
With a bright sympathetic ka-bob in his eye.

151

Stern duty compelled him to leave her one day—
(A ship's supercargo was brave ALUM BEY)—
To pretty young BACKSHEESH he made a salaam,
And sailed to the isle of Seringapatam.

"O ALUM," said she, "think again, ere you go—
Hareems may arise and Moguls they may blow;
You may strike on a fez, or be drowned, which is wuss!"
But ALUM embraced her and spoke to her thus:

"Cease weeping, fair BACKSHEESH! I willingly swear
Cork jackets and trousers I always will wear,
And I also throw in a large number of oaths
That I never—no, *never*—will take off my clothes!"

They left Madagascar away on their right,
And made Clapham Common the following night,
Then lay on their oars for a fortnight or two,
Becalmed in the ocean of Honolulu.

One day ALUM saw, with alarm in his breast,
A cloud on the nor-sow-sow-nor-sow-nor-west;
The wind it arose, and the crew gave a scream,
For they knew it—they knew it!—the dreaded Hareem!!

The mast it went over, and so did the sails,
Brave ALUM threw over his casks and his bales;
The billows arose as the weather grew thick,
And all except ALUM were terribly sick.

The crew were but three, but they holloa'd for nine,
They howled and they blubbered with wail and with whine:

The skipper he fainted away in the fore,
For he hadn't the heart for to skip any more.

"Ho, coward!" said ALUM, "with heart of a child!
Thou son of a party whose grave is defiled!
Is ALUM in terror? is ALUM afeard?
Ho! ho! If you had one I'd laugh at your beard."

His eyeball it gleamed like a furnace of coke;
He boldly inflated his clothes as he spoke;
He daringly felt for the corks on his chest,
And he recklessly tightened the belt at his breast.

For he knew, the brave ALUM, that, happen what might,
With belts and cork-jacketing, *he* was all right;
Though others might sink, he was certain to swim—
No Hareem whatever had terrors for him!

They begged him to spare from his personal store
A single cork garment—they asked for no more;
But he couldn't, because of the number of oaths
That he never—no, never!—would take off his clothes.

The billows dash o'er them and topple around,
They see they are pretty near sure to be drowned.
A terrible wave o'er the quarter-deck breaks,
And the vessel it sinks in a couple of shakes!

The dreadful Hareem, though it knows how to blow,
Expends all its strength in a minute or so;
When the vessel had foundered, as I have detailed,
The tempest subsided, and quiet prevailed.

One seized on a cork with a yelling "Ha! ha!"
(Its bottle had 'prisoned a pint of Pacha)—
Another a toothpick—another a tray—
"Alas! it is useless!" said brave ALUM BEY.

"To holloa and kick is a very bad plan:
Get it over, my tulips, as soon as you can;
You'd better lay hold of a good lump of lead,
And cling to it tightly until you are dead.

"Just raise your hands over your pretty heads—so—
Right down to the bottom you're certain to go.
Ta! ta! I'm afraid we shall not meet again"—
For the truly courageous are truly humane.

Brave ALUM was picked up the very next day—
A man-o'-war sighted him smoking away;
With hunger and cold he was ready to drop,
So they sent him below and they gave him a chop.

O reader, or readress, whichever you be,
You weep for the crew who have sunk in the sea?
O reader, or readress, read farther, and dry
The bright sympathetic ka-bob in your eye.

That ship had a grapple with three iron spikes—
It's lowered, and, ha! on a something it strikes!
They haul it aboard with a British "Heave-ho!"
And what it has fished the drawing will show.

There was WILSON, and PARKER, and TOMLINSON, too—
(The first was the captain, the others the crew)—
As lively and spry as a Malabar ape,
Quite pleased and surprised at their happy escape.

And ALUM, brave fellow, who stood in the fore,
And never expected to look on them more,
Was really delighted to see them again,
For the truly courageous are truly humane.

W. S. GILBERT

Under
the Sea

A Sea Dirge

Full fathom five thy father lies;
    Of his bones are coral made;
Those are pearls that were his eyes:
    Nothing of him that doth fade
But doth suffer a sea change
Into something rich and strange.
Sea nymphs hourly ring his knell:
    Hark! now I hear them—
    Ding, dong, bell.

WILLIAM SHAKESPEARE

The Forsaken Merman

Come, dear children, let us away;
    Down and away below.
Now my brothers call from the bay;
Now the great winds shorewards blow;
Now the salt tides seaward flow;
Now the wild white horses play,
Champ and chafe and toss in the spray.
    Children dear, let us away.
      This way, this way.

Call her once before you go.
    Call once yet,
In a voice that she will know:
    "Margaret! Margaret!"
Children's voices should be dear
(Call once more) to a mother's ear:
Children's voices wild with pain,
    Surely she will come again.

Call her once, and come away,
    This way, this way.
"Mother dear, we cannot stay!"
The wild white horses foam and fret.
    "Margaret! Margaret!"

Come, dear children, come away down.
        Call no more.
One last look at the white-walled town,
And the little gray church on the windy shore.
    Then come down.
She will not come, though you call all day.
    Come away, come away.

Children dear, was it yesterday
We heard the sweet bells over the bay?
In the caverns where we lay,
Through the surf and through the swell,
The far-off sound of a silver bell?
Sand-strewn caverns, cool and deep,
Where the winds are all asleep;
Where the spent lights quiver and gleam;
Where the salt weed sways in the stream;
Where the sea beasts, ranged all round,
Feed in the ooze of their pasture ground;
Where the sea snakes coil and twine,
Dry their mail and bask in the brine;
Where great whales come sailing by,
Sail and sail, with unshut eye,
Round the world forever and aye?
    When did music come this way?
    Children dear, was it yesterday?

Children dear, was it yesterday
(Call yet once) that she went away?
Once she sat with you and me,
On a red-gold throne in the heart of the sea,
And the youngest sat on her knee.
She combed its bright hair, and she tended it well,
When down swung the sound of the far-off bell.
She sighed, she looked up through the clear green sea,
She said, "I must go, for my kinsfolk pray
In the little gray church on the shore today.
'Twill be Easter time in the world—ah me!
And I lose my poor soul, Merman, here with thee."
I said, "Go up, dear heart, through the waves:
Say thy prayer, and come back to the kind sea caves."
She smiled, she went up through the surf in the bay,
Children dear, was it yesterday?

Children dear, were we long alone?
"The sea grows stormy, the little ones moan;
Long prayers," I said, "in the world they say."
"Come," I said, and we rose through the surf in the bay.
We went up the beach, by the sandy down
Where the sea stocks bloom, to the white-walled town,
Through the narrow paved streets, where all was still,
To the little gray church on the windy hill.
From the church came a murmur of folk at their prayers,
But we stood without in the cold blowing airs.
We climbed on the graves, on the stones worn with rains,
And we gazed up the aisle through the small leaded panes.
She sat by the pillar; we saw her clear:
"Margaret, hist! come quick, we are here.

Dear heart," I said, "we are alone.
The sea grows stormy, the little ones moan."
But, ah, she gave me never a look,
For her eyes were sealed to the holy book.
Loud prays the priest; shut stands the door.
    Come away, children, call no more,
    Come away, come down, call no more.

Down, down, down,
    Down to the depths of the sea.
She sits at her wheel in the humming town,
    Singing most joyfully.
Hark what she sings: "O joy, O joy,
For the humming street, and the child with its toy!
For the priest, and the bell, and the holy well,
    For the wheel where I spun,
    And the blessed light of the sun!"
    And so she sings her fill,
    Singing most joyfully,
    Till the shuttle falls from her hand,
    And the whizzing wheel stands still.
She steals to the window, and looks at the sand,
    And over the sand at the sea;
    And her eyes are set in a stare;
    And anon there breaks a sigh,
    And anon there drops a tear,
    From a sorrow-clouded eye,
    And a heart sorrow-laden,
      A long, long sigh,
For the cold strange eyes of a little Mermaiden,
And the gleam of her golden hair.

Come away, away, children,
Come, children, come down.
The hoarse wind blows coldly,
Lights shine in the town.
She will start from her slumber
When gusts shake the door;
She will hear the winds howling,
Will hear the waves roar.
We shall see, while above us
The waves roar and whirl,
A ceiling of amber,
A pavement of pearl—
Singing, "Here came a mortal,
But faithless was she,
And alone dwell forever
The kings of the sea."

But, children, at midnight,
When soft the winds blow,
When clear falls the moonlight,
When spring tides are low;
When sweet airs come seaward
From heaths starred with broom;
And high rocks throw mildly
On the blanched sands a gloom:
Up the still, glistening beaches,
Up the creeks we will hie;
Over banks of bright seaweed
The ebb tide leaves dry.
We will gaze, from the sand hills,
At the white, sleeping town;

At the church on the hillside—
And then come back, down.
Singing, "There dwells a loved one,
But cruel is she:
She left lonely forever
The kings of the sea."

MATTHEW ARNOLD

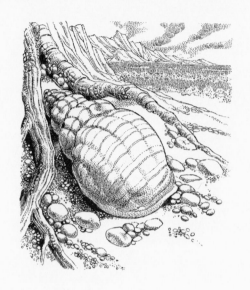

Frutta di Mare

I am a sea shell flung
Up from the ancient sea;
Now I lie here, among
Roots of a tamarisk tree;
No one listens to me.

I sing to myself all day
In a husky voice, quite low,
Things the great fishes say
And you must need to know;
All night I sing just so.

But lift me from the ground,
And hearken at my rim;
Only your sorrow's sound
Amazed, perplexed and dim,
Comes coiling to the brim;

For what the wise whales ponder
Awaking out from sleep,
The key to all your wonder,
The answers of the deep,
These to myself I keep.

GEOFFREY SCOTT

Undersea Fever

Up tails all! Down and under!
   It's time to pursue a new natural wonder;
They're putting on flippers from Key West to Darien,
   And every young blood is an oxygenarian.

        Hark, hark, the shark!
        What ho, the blowfish!
     (This is how fishermen in the know fish.)
        Egad, a shad!
        Shalom, a jewfish!
    Off with the old and on with the new fish.

Fish with a blunt nose, fish with a thin nose,
   In sizes encompassing whales down to minnows.
There are no tangled fishlines, no vicious hooks about,
   And it's one of the easiest things to write books about!

My God, a scrod!
Hip, hip a rayfish!
Some are exotic, some plain everyday fish.
Look sharp, a carp!
Hand me that starfish;
I can hardly believe that some of them *are* fish!

Off on a fish walk! It's not hard to vary 'em;
Every three minutes a brand-new aquarium.
How diverse is the deep, which was heretofore manless,
Where swims the anchovy, unsalted and canless.

Some place, a dace!
En garde, a swordfish!
Some frightfully shy and some awfully toward fish.
Land's sake, a hake!
How sad, a weakfish!
Some fresh from the roe and some truly antique fish.

Everest's climbed, there's no fun in spelunking,
So slip on your snorkel, everyone's dunking;
(But full fathom five, include *me* minus;
I'll sit in the rowboat, alone with my sinus.)

WILLIAM COLE

Cape Horn Gospel

"I was in a hooker once," said Karlssen,
"And Bill, as was a seaman, died,
So we lashed him in an old tarpaulin
And tumbled him across the side;
And the fun of it was that all his gear was
Divided up among the crew
Before that blushing human error,
Our crawling little captain, knew.

"On the passage home one morning
(As certain as I prays for grace)
There was old Bill's shadder a-hauling
At the weather mizzen-topsail brace.

He was all grown green with seaweed,
He was all lashed up and shored;
So I says to him, I says, 'Why, Billy!
What's a-bringin' of you back aboard?'

" 'I'm a-weary of them there mermaids,'
Says old Bill's ghost to me;
'It ain't no place for a Christian
Below there—under sea.
For it's all blown sand and shipwrecks,
And old bones eaten bare,
And them cold fishy females
With long green weeds for hair.' "

JOHN MASEFIELD

The Anchorage

Fifteen or twenty feet below,
The little fish come creeping round the anchor chain.
I could not have it quieter now,
Not anywhere; nor could there be less movement
Anywhere at all, than here.

The bay moves on into night.
The shadows come to watch and wait in every hollow
Till they have gathered-in all.
But Moon comes over the rocks; she lights the little fall
And rise and fall at the beach.

Deep water, deep bay
So still and calm for one whole night in the southeast
That day has never come,
And I am still upon my knees out on the stern,
And you and I still watch
Down twenty, thirty feet below.

PAT WILSON

Jonah

A cream of phosphorescent light
Floats on the wash that to and fro
Slides round his feet—enough to show
Many a pendulous stalactite
Of naked mucus, whorls and wreaths
And huge festoons of mottled tripes
And smaller palpitating pipes
Through which a yeasty liquor seethes.

Seated upon the convex mound
Of one vast kidney, Jonah prays
And sings his canticles and hymns,
Making the hollow vault resound
God's goodness and mysterious ways,
Till the great fish spouts music as he swims.

ALDOUS HUXLEY

Sam

When Sam goes back in memory,
It is to where the sea
Breaks on the shingle, emerald-green
In white foam, endlessly;
He says—with small brown eye on mine—
"I used to keep awake,
And lean from my window in the moon,
Watching those billows break.
And half a million tiny hands,
And eyes, like sparks of frost,
Would dance and come tumbling into the moon,
On every breaker tossed.
And all across from star to star,
I've seen the watery sea,
With not a single ship in sight,
Just ocean there, and me;

And heard my father snore . . . And once,
As sure as I'm alive,
Out of those wallowing, moon-flecked waves
I saw a mermaid dive;
Head and shoulder above the wave,
Plain as now I see you,
Combing her hair, now back, now front,
Her two eyes peeping through;
Calling me, *Sam!*—quietlike—*Sam!* . . .
But me . . . I never went,
Making believe I kind of thought
'Twas someone else she meant . . .
Wonderful lovely there she sat,
Singing the night away,
All in the solitudinous sea
Of that there lonely bay.
P'raps," and he'd smooth his hairless mouth,
"P'raps, if 'twere now, my son,
P'raps, if I heard a voice say, *Sam!* . . .
Morning would find me gone."

WALTER DE LA MARE

Dolphins at Cochin

I

They crashed among the spider nets
spluttering and breathing hoarsely,
chasing fish out of the water,
calling one another and disappearing.

Lime-green bellies and smiling mouths
sliced upwards obliquely; calm humorous eyes
regarded us for a moment
and splashed back.

Sea-marks of dolphins moved
among the dozens of jockeying sails; a mile out,
in the breaking waves, we could see
the flash of more dolphins.

II

On the bridge of our tanker the gray paint
blistered in the heat; above us
the siren mooed to come in at the jetty;
the water green and translucent.

The smell of crude oil, of ginger
drying in the yards; piles of colored fish;
the creak of a wooden capstan; monkeys
quarreling on top of parked cars.

And suddenly there was a dolphin
inside our slow bow-wave, revolving, amused,
not realizing our incomprehension
of his vivid thoughts.

III

Two dolphins came skidding round the point,
screeched to a standstill
blowing vapor and circling each other,
then they raced on again, leaping.

We watched them helplessly
from our primitive element,
able only to think up cold metaphors
or to anthropomorphize.

But they wheeled: dolphins!
their liquid backs, their arched fins
moving steadily out from the shore
into the hilarious ocean.

TOM BUCHAN

The Silver Fish

While fishing in the blue lagoon,
I caught a lovely silver fish,
And he spoke to me, "My boy," quoth he,
"Please set me free and I'll grant your wish;
A kingdom of wisdom? A palace of gold?
Or all the fancies your mind can hold?"
And I said, "O.K.," and I set him free,
But he laughed at me as he swam away,
And left me whispering my wish
Into a silent sea.

Today I caught that fish again
(That lovely silver prince of fishes),
And once again he offered me,
If I would only set him free,
Any one of a number of wishes,
If I would throw him back to the fishes.

He was delicious!

SHEL SILVERSTEIN

An Inscription by the Sea

(After a poem in the *Greek Anthology*)

No dust have I to cover me,
    My grave no man may show;
My tomb is this unending sea,
    And I lie far below.
My fate, O stranger, was to drown;
And where it was the ship went down
    Is what the sea birds know.

EDWIN ARLINGTON ROBINSON

Sea
Stories

Hervé Riel

I

On the sea and at the Hogue, sixteen hundred ninety-two,
   Did the English fight the French—woe to France!
And, the thirty-first of May, helter-skelter through the blue,
Like a crowd of frightened porpoises a shoal of sharks pursue,
   Came crowding ship on ship to Saint-Malo on the Rance,
With the English fleet in view.

II

'Twas the squadron that escaped, with the victor in full chase;
   First and foremost of the drove, in his great ship, Damfreville;
     Close on him fled, great and small,
     Twenty-two good ships in all;
And they signaled to the place
"Help the winners of a race!
   Get us guidance, give us harbor, take us quick—or, quicker still,
   Here's the English can and will!"

III

Then the pilots of the place put out brisk and leapt on board;
 "Why, what hope or chance have ships like these to pass!" laughed they:
"Rocks to starboard, rocks to port, all the passage scarred and scored—
Shall the *Formidable* here, with her twelve-and-eighty guns,
 Think to make the river-mouth by the single narrow way,
Trust to enter—where 'tis ticklish for a craft of twenty tons,
  And with flow at full beside?
  Now, 'tis slackest ebb of tide.
  Reach the mooring? Rather say,
While rock stands or water runs,
 Not a ship will leave the bay!"

IV

Then was called a council straight.
Brief and bitter the debate:
"Here's the English at our heels; would you have them take in tow
All that's left us of the fleet, linked together stern and bow,
For a prize to Plymouth Sound?
Better run the ships aground!"
 (Ended Damfreville his speech).
"Not a minute more to wait!
 Let the Captains all and each
 Shove ashore, then blow up, burn the vessels on the beach!
France must undergo her fate.

V

"Give the word!" But no such word
Was ever spoke or heard;
 For up stood, for out stepped, for in struck amid all these
—A Captain? A Lieutenant? A Mate—first, second, third?

184

No such man of mark, and meet
With his betters to compete!
But a simple Breton sailor pressed by Tourville for the fleet,
A poor coasting pilot he, Hervé Riel the Croisickese.

VI

And "What mockery or malice have we here?" cries Hervé Riel:
    "Are you mad, you Malouins? Are you cowards, fools, or rogues?
Talk to me of rocks and shoals, me who took the soundings, tell
On my fingers every bank, every shallow, every swell
    'Twixt the offing here and Grève where the river disembogues?
Are you bought by English gold? Is it love the lying's for?
        Morn and eve, night and day,
        Have I piloted your bay,
Entered free and anchored fast at the foot of Solidor.
    Burn the fleet and ruin France? That were worse than fifty Hogues!
    Sirs, they know I speak the truth! Sirs, believe me there's a way!
Only let me lead the line,
    Have the biggest ship to steer,
    Get this *Formidable* clear,
Make the others follow mine,
And I lead them, most and least, by a passage I know well,
    Right to Solidor past Grève,
    And there lay them safe and sound;
    And if one ship misbehave,
    Keel so much as grate the ground,
Why, I've nothing but my life—here's my head!" cries Hervé Riel.

VII

Not a minute more to wait.
"Steer us in, then, small and great!

185

Take the helm, lead the line, save the squadron!" cried its chief.
Captains, give the sailor place!
   He is Admiral, in brief.
Still the north wind, by God's grace!
See the noble fellow's face
As the big ship, with a bound,
Clears the entry like a hound,
Keeps the passage, as its inch of way were the wide sea's profound!
   See, safe thro' shoal and rock,
   How they follow in a flock,
Not a ship that misbehaves, not a keel that grates the ground,
   Not a spar that comes to grief!
The peril, see, is past.
All are harbored to the last,
And just as Hervé Riel hollas "Anchor!"—sure as fate,
Up the English come—too late!

VIII

So, the storm subsides to calm:
   They see the green trees wave
   On the heights o'erlooking Grève.
Hearts that bled are stanched with balm.
"Just our rapture to enhance,
   Let the English rake the bay,
Gnash their teeth and glare askance
   As they cannonade away!
'Neath rampired Solidor pleasant riding on the Rance!"
How hope succeeds despair on each Captain's countenance!
Out burst all with one accord,
   "This is Paradise for Hell!
      Let France, let France's King

186

Thank the man that did the thing!"
What a shout, and all one word,
   "Hervé Riel!"
As he stepped in front once more,
   Not a symptom of surprise
   In the frank blue Breton eyes,
Just the same man as before.

IX

Then said Damfreville, "My friend,
I must speak out at the end,
   Though I find the speaking hard.
Praise is deeper than the lips:
You have saved the King his ships,
   You must name your own reward.
'Faith, our sun was near eclipse!
Demand whate'er you will,
France remains your debtor still.
Ask to heart's content and have! or my name's not Damfreville."

X

Then a beam of fun outbroke
On the bearded mouth that spoke,
As the honest heart laughed through
Those frank eyes of Breton blue:
"Since I needs must say my say,
   Since on board the duty's done,
   And from Malo Roads to Croisic Point, what is it but a run?—
Since 'tis ask and have, I may—
   Since the others go ashore—
Come! A good whole holiday!

Leave to go and see my wife, whom I call the Belle Aurore!"
That he asked and that he got—nothing more.

XI

Name and deed alike are lost:
Not a pillar nor a post
  In his Croisic keeps alive the feat as it befell;
Not a head in white and black
On a single fishing smack,
In memory of the man but for whom had gone to wrack
  All that France saved from the fight whence England bore the bell.
Go to Paris: rank on rank
  Search the heroes flung pell-mell
On the Louvre, face and flank!
  You shall look long enough ere you come to Hervé Riel.
So, for better and for worse,
Hervé Riel, accept my verse!
In my verse, Hervé Riel, do thou once more
Save the squadron, honor France, love thy wife the Belle Aurore!

ROBERT BROWNING

188

Noah an' Jonah
an' Cap'n John Smith

Noah an' Jonah an' Cap'n John Smith,
Mariners, travelers, magazines of myth,
Settin' up in Heaven, chewin' and a-chawin'
Eatin' their terbaccy, talkin' and a-jawin';
Settin' by a crick, spittin' in the worter,
Talkin' tall an' tactless, as saints hadn't orter,
Lollin' in the shade, baitin' hooks and anglin',
Occasionally friendly, occasionally wranglin'.

Noah took his halo from his old bald head
An' swatted of a hoppergrass an' knocked it dead,
An' he baited of his hook, an' he spoke an' said:
"When I was the Skipper of the tight leetle Ark
I useter fish fer porpus, useter fish fer shark,
Often I have ketched in a single hour on Monday
Sharks enough to feed the fambly till Sunday—
To feed all the sarpints, the tigers an' donkeys,
To feed all the zebras, the insects an' monkeys,
To feed all the varmints, bears an' gorillars,
To feed all the camels, cats an' armadillers,
To give all the pelicans stews for their gizzards,
To feed all the owls an' catamounts an' lizards,
To feed all the humans, their babies an' their nusses,
To feed all the houn' dawgs an' hippopotamusses,
To feed all the oxens, feed all the asses,
Feed all the bison an' leetle hoppergrasses—
Always I ketched, in half a hour on Monday
All that the fambly could gormandize till Sunday!"

Jonah took his harp, to strum and to string her,
An' Cap'n John Smith teched his nose with his finger.
Cap'n John Smith, he hemmed some an' hawed some,
An' he bit off a chaw, an' he chewed some and chawed some:
"When I was to China, when I was to Guinea,
When I was to Java, an' also in Verginney,
I teached all the natives how to be ambitious,
I learned 'em my trick of ketchin' devilfishes.
I've fitten tigers, I've fitten bears,
I have fitten sarpints an' wolves in their lairs,
I have fit with wild men an' hippopotamusses,

But the perilousest varmints is the bloody octopusses!
I'd rub my forehead with phosphorescent light
An' plunge into the ocean an' seek 'em out at night!
I ketched 'em in grottoes, I ketched 'em in caves,
I used fer to strangle 'em underneath the waves!
When they seen the bright light blazin' on my forehead
They used ter to rush at me, screamin' something horrid!
Tentacles wavin', teeth white an' gnashin',
Hollerin' an' bellerin', wallerin' an' splashin'!
I useter grab 'em as they rushed from their grots,
Ketch all their legs an' tie 'em into knots!"

Noah looked at Jonah, an' said not a word,
But if winks made noises, a wink had been heard.
Jonah took the hook from a mudcat's middle
An' strummed on the strings of his hallelujah fiddle,
Jonah give his whiskers a backhand wipe
An' cut some plug terbaccer an' crammed it in his pipe!
—(Noah an' Jonah an' Cap'n John Smith,
Fisherman an' travelers, narreratin' myth,
Settin' up in Heaven all eternity,
Fishin' in the shade, contented as could be!
Spittin' their terbaccer in the little shaded creek,
Stoppin' of their yarns fer ter hear the ripples speak!
I hope fer Heaven, when I think of this—
You folks bound hellward, a lot of fun you'll miss!)

Jonah, he decapitates that mudcat's head;
An' gets his pipe ter drawin'; an' this is what he said:
"Excuse me ef your stories don't excite me much!
Excuse me ef I seldom agitate fer such!

191

You think yer fishermen! I won't argue none!
I won't even tell yer the half o' what I done!
You has careers dangerous an' checkered!
All as I will say is: Go and read my record!
You think yer fishermen! You think yer great!
All I asks is this: Has one of ye been *'bait?*
Cap'n Noah, Cap'n John, I heerd when ye hollered;
What I asks is this: Has one of ye been *swallered?*
It's mighty purty fishin' with little hooks an' reels.
It's mighty easy fishin' with little rods an' creels.
It's mighty pleasant ketchin' mudcats fer yer dinners.
But this here is my challenge fer saints an' fer sinners,
Which one of ye has v'yaged in a varmint's inners?
When I seen a big fish, tough as Methooslum,
I used for to dive into his oozly-goozlum!
When I seen the strong fish, wallopin' like a lummicks,
I useter foller 'em, dive into their stummicks!
I could v'yage an' steer 'em, I could understand 'em,
I useter navigate 'em, I useter land 'em!
Don't you pester *me* with any more narration!
Go git famous! Git a reputation!"

—Cap'n John he grinned his hat brim beneath,
Clicked his tongue of silver on his golden teeth;
Noah an' Jonah an' Cap'n John Smith,
Strummin' golden harps, narreratin' myth!
Settin' by the shallows forever an' forever,
Swappin' yarns an' fishin' in a little river!

Don Marquis

192

The *Golden Vanity*

There was a ship sailed from the North Countree
And the name of the ship was the *Golden Vanity,*
And she feared she would be taken by the Spanish enemy
As she sailed upon the Lowlands, Lowlands, Lowlands,
As she sailed upon the Lowlands Sea.

Then up there spoke a little cabin boy
And he said to the Captain, "What will you give to me
If I swim right up to the Spanish enemy
And sink her in the Lowlands, Lowlands, Lowlands,
And sink her in the Lowlands Sea?"

"Oh, I will give you silver, and I will give you gold
And my fair young daughter your bride to be
If you swim right up to the Spanish enemy
And sink her in the Lowlands, Lowlands, Lowlands,
And sink her in the Lowlands Sea."

193

Then down from the chains the cabin boy jumped he
And he swam alongside of the Spanish enemy,
And in her side he bore holes three
And he sank her in the Lowlands, Lowlands, Lowlands,
He sank her in the Lowlands Sea.

He swam to the port side and called out clear and true,
"I've sunk the Spanish enemy for you,"
But the Captain turned away, for his promise he did rue,
And he left him in the Lowlands, Lowlands, Lowlands,
He left him in the Lowlands Sea.

And then he swam back to the starboard side
And cold in the water, he had nearly died
Saying, "Messmates pull me up, for I'm drifting with the tide
That's running in the Lowlands, Lowlands, Lowlands,
That's running in the Lowlands Sea."

So his messmates pulled him up, but on the deck he died
And they wrapped him in his hammock that was both long and wide,
And they threw him overboard, and he drifted with the tide,
Till he sank in the Lowlands, Lowlands, Lowlands,
He sank in the Lowlands Sea.

ANONYMOUS BALLAD

Rousecastle

Pete Rousecastle the sailor's son
From the Isle of Anglesey
Facing to the West,
Tired of the concave undercolored sky

And of the landscapes heights afford,
Valleys, land-swelling plains,
And to be free of all
Familiar natural aspects, mountain chains,

River abysms, waterfalls,
And archipelagos,
Looked on the sea
Folding her waves like an unfolding rose.

Pete Rousecastle the sailor's son
Heard from no siren throat
The baffled, low,
Endearing, murmurous, and glutted note

Thrown by the sea to all her own.
Indeed Rousecastle saw
Only the flat
Discontinuation of a local shore.

As he walked down to the mud beach
His heart was light with an idea,
And on the horizon
Which hid beneath its straight line Africa,

The sea's familiar seaports, and
Landfalls, fixed staring eyes,
Continued on
His chosen path. The waters round him rise;

The small waves buffet him, and cling
His blue jeans jacket to his breast;
Still he walks down
The bed of ocean until the topmost

Hair of his head is under sea.
Rousecastle, sailor's son,
Now down, deep down
The hungry sea that saw his father drown,

Visits the plains of the ocean,
The glimmering country
Darker than tombs,
And unfamiliar angles of the under sea.

DAVID WRIGHT

Industrious

Carpenter Dan

An honest man what loves his trade
　　Deserves me honest grip;
And Carpenter Dan was a handy man
　　To have about a ship.

The things he couldn't hammer up
　　Them things he hammered down;
He sawed the rails and spliced the sails
　　And done his bizness brown.

He scroll-sawed all the masts and spars
　　And varnished 'em with ile,
Then he shingled the poop of our gallant sloop
　　With a gable, Queen Anne style.

Along the basement porthole sills
　　He worked for hours and hours
A-building tiers of jardineers
　　And planting 'em with flowers.

He filled the deck with rustic seats
  And many a grapevine swing—
Yes, a handy man was Carpenter Dan,
  For he thought of everything.

Then pretty soon he got a scheme
  To ease the Capting's cares,
So he fitted the sloop with a fine front stoop,
  With rugs and Morris chairs.

And there we sat a-drinking tea,
  The Capting and his crew,
When we heard arise, to our great surprise,
  A nawful hulleroo.

The Capting looked across the rail
  And sort of chawed his lip—
For Carpenter Dan was building an
  Extension to the ship!

"Avast there, Dan!" the Capting cried,
  "What have you gone to do?"
"Don't bother me, man," said Carpenter Dan,
  "I'm fixing things for you."

Then he toe-nailed on a rafter beam
  And sawed a two-by-four;
Then he gave a yank to a six-inch plank
  And started on the floor.

So Dan he worked three solid weeks
    Till on a happy day,
A double craft with a Queen Anne aft,
    We sailed into the bay.

And from that bonny lean-to boat
    We vowed no more to roam;
From window panes to weather vanes
    We loved our floating home.

And as we sat among the vines
    On many an ocean trip
We vowed that Dan was a handy man
    To have about the ship.

WALLACE IRWIN

Flannan Isle

"Though three men dwell on Flannan Isle
To keep the lamp alight,
As we steered under the lee, we caught
No glimmer through the night."—

A passing ship at dawn had brought
The news; and quickly we set sail,
To find out what strange thing might ail
The keepers of the deep-sea light.

The winter day broke blue and bright,
With glancing sun and glancing spray,

While o'er the swell our boat made way,
As gallant as a gull in flight.

But as we neared the lonely Isle,
And looked up at the naked height,
And saw the lighthouse towering white,
With blinded lantern, that all night
Had never shot a spark
Of comfort through the dark,
So ghostly in the cold sunlight
It seemed, that we were struck the while
With wonder all too dread for words.

And as into the tiny creek
We stole beneath the hanging crag,
We saw three queer, black, ugly birds—
Too big, by far, in my belief,
For cormorant or shag—
Like seamen sitting bolt-upright
Upon a half-tide reef:
But, as we neared, they plunged from sight,
Without a sound, or spurt of white.

And still too mazed to speak,
We landed; and made fast the boat;
And climbed the track in single file,
Each wishing he were safe afloat,
On any sea, however far,
So it be far from Flannan Isle:
And still we seemed to climb, and climb,
As though we'd lost all count of time,
And so must climb for evermore.

Yet, all too soon, we reached the door
The black, sun-blistered lighthouse door,
That gaped for us ajar.

As, on the threshold, for a spell,
We paused, we seemed to breathe the smell
Of limewash and of tar,
Familiar as our daily breath,
As though 'twere some strange scent of death:
And so, yet wondering, side by side,
We stood a moment, still tongue-tied:
And each with black foreboding eyed
The door, ere we should fling it wide,
To leave the sunlight for the gloom:
Till, plucking courage up, at last,
Hard on each other's heels we passed,
Into the living room.

Yet, as we crowded through the door,
We only saw a table, spread
For dinner, meat and cheese and bread;
But, all untouched, and no one there!
As though, when they sat down to eat,
Ere they could even taste,
Alarm had come; and they in haste
Had risen and left the bread and meat,
For at the table-head a chair
Lay tumbled on the floor.

We listened; but we only heard
The feeble cheeping of a bird
That starved upon its perch:

202

And, listening still, without a word,
We set about our hopeless search.

We hunted high, we hunted low;
And soon ransacked the empty house;
Then o'er the Island, to and fro,
We ranged, to listen and to look
In every cranny, cleft or nook
That might have hid a bird or mouse:
But, though we searched from shore to shore
We found no sign in any place:
And soon again stood face to face
Before the gaping door:
And stole into the room once more
As frightened children steal.
Aye: though we hunted high and low,
And hunted everywhere,
Of the three men's fate we found no trace
Of any kind in any place,
But a door ajar, and an untouched meal,
And an overtoppled chair.

And as we listened in the gloom
Of that forsaken living room—
A chill clutch on our breath—
We thought how ill-chance came to all
Who kept the Flannan Light:
And how the rock had been the death
Of many a likely lad:
How six had come to a sudden end,
And three had gone stark mad:
And one whom we'd all known as friend

Had leapt from the lantern one still night
And fallen dead by the lighthouse wall:
And long we thought
On the three we sought,
And of what might yet befall.

Like curs a glance has brought to heel,
We listened, flinching there:
And looked, and looked, on the untouched meal,
And the overtoppled chair.

We seemed to stand for an endless while,
Though still no word was said,
Three men alive on Flannan Isle,
Who thought on three men dead.

WILFRID GIBSON

The Three Fishers

Three fishers went sailing out into the west—
  Out into the west as the sun went down;
Each thought of the woman who loved him the best,
  And the children stood watching them out of the town;
For men must work, and women must weep;
And there's little to earn, and many to keep,
    Though the harbor bar be moaning.

Three wives sat up in the lighthouse tower,
  And trimmed the lamps as the sun went down;
And they looked at the squall, and they looked at the shower,
  And the rack it came rolling up, ragged and brown;
But men must work, and women must weep,
Though storms be sudden, and waters deep,
    And the harbor bar be moaning.

Three corpses lay out on the shining sands
   In the morning gleam as the tide went down,
And the women are watching and wringing their hands,
   For those who will never come back to the town;
For men must work, and women must weep—
And the sooner it's over, the sooner to sleep—
   And good-by to the bar and its moaning.

CHARLES KINGSLEY

Christmas at Sea

The sheets were frozen hard, and they cut the naked hand;
The decks were like a slide, where a seaman scarce could stand;
The wind was a nor'wester, blowing squally off the sea;
And cliffs and spouting breakers were the only things a-lee.

They heard the surf a-roaring before the break of day;
But 'twas only with the peep of light we saw how ill we lay.
We tumbled every hand on deck instanter, with a shout,
And we gave her the maintops'l, and stood by to go about.

All day we tacked and tacked between the South Head and the North;
All day we hauled the frozen sheets, and got no further forth;
All day as cold as charity, in bitter pain and dread,
For very life and nature we tacked from head to head.

We gave the South a wider berth, for there the tide race roared;
But every tack we made we brought the North Head close aboard:
So's we saw the cliffs and houses, and the breakers running high,
And the coastguard in his garden, with his glass against his eye.

The frost was on the village roofs as white as ocean foam;
The good red fires were burning bright in every 'long-shore home;
The windows sparkled clear, and the chimneys volleyed out;
And I vow we sniffed the victuals as the vessel went about.

The bells upon the church were rung with a mighty jovial cheer;
For it's just that I should tell you how (of all days in the year)
This day of our adversity was blessèd Christmas morn,
And the house above the coastguard's was the house where I was born.

O well I saw the pleasant room, the pleasant faces there,
My mother's silver spectacles, my father's silver hair;
And well I saw the firelight, like a flight of homely elves,
Go dancing round the china plates that stand upon the shelves.

And well I knew the talk they had, the talk that was of me,
Of the shadow on the household and the son that went to sea;
And O the wicked fool I seemed, in every kind of way,
To be here and hauling frozen ropes on blessèd Christmas Day.

They lit the high sea-light, and the dark began to fall.
"All hands to loose topgallant sails," I heard the captain call.
"By the Lord, she'll never stand it," our first mate, Jackson, cried.
. . . "It's the one way or the other, Mr. Jackson," he replied.

208

She staggered to her bearings, but the sails were new and good,
And the ship smelt up to windward just as though she understood.
As the winter's day was ending, in the entry of the night,
We cleared the weary headland, and passed below the light.

And they heaved a mighty breath, every soul on board but me,
As they saw her nose again pointing handsome out to sea;
But all that I could think of, in the darkness and the cold,
Was just that I was leaving home and my folks were growing old.

ROBERT LOUIS STEVENSON

Mulholland's Contract

The fear was on the cattle, for the gale was on the sea,
An' the pens broke up on the lower deck an' let the creatures free—
An' the lights went out on the lower deck, an' no one down but me.

I had been singin' to them to keep 'em quiet there,
For the lower deck is the dangerousest, requirin' constant care,
An' give to me as the strongest man, though used to drink and swear.

I see my chance was certain of bein' horned or trod,
For the lower deck was packed with steers thicker 'n peas in a pod,
An' more pens broke at every roll—so I made a Contract with God.
An' by the terms of the Contract, as I have read the same,
If He got me to port alive I would exalt His name,
An' praise His Holy Majesty till further orders came.

He saved me from the cattle an' He saved me from the sea,
For they found me 'tween two drownded ones where the roll had landed me—
An' a four-inch crack on top of my head, as crazy as could be.

But that were done by a stanchion, an' not by a bullock at all,
An' I lay still for seven weeks convalessing of the fall,
An' readin' the shiny Scripture texts in the Seamen's Hospital.

An' I spoke to God of our Contract, an' He says to my prayer:
"I never puts on My ministers no more than they can bear.
So back you go to the cattle boats an' preach My Gospel there.

"For human life is chancy at any kind of trade,
But most of all, as well you know, when the steers are mad-afraid;
So you go back to the cattle boats an' preach 'em as I've said.

"They must quit drinkin' an' swearin', they mustn't knife on a blow,
They must quit gamblin' their wages, and you must preach it so;
For now those boats are more like Hell than anything else I know."

I didn't want to do it, for I knew what I should get,
An' I wanted to preach Religion, handsome an' out of the wet,
But the Word of the Lord were lain on me, an' I done what I was set.

I have been smit an' bruisèd, as warned would be the case,
An' turned my cheek to the smiter exactly as Scripture says;
But following that, I knocked him down an' led him up to Grace.

An' we have preaching on Sundays whenever the sea is calm,
An' I use no knife nor pistol an' I never take no harm,
For the Lord abideth back of me to guide my fighting arm.

An' I sign for four pound ten a month and save the money clear,
An' I am in charge of the lower deck, an' I never lose a steer;
An' I believe in Almighty God an' I preach His Gospel here.

The skippers say I'm crazy, but I can prove 'em wrong,
For I am in charge of the lower deck with all that doth belong—
Which they would not give to a lunatic, and the competition so strong!

RUDYARD KIPLING

Old Gray Squirrel

A great while ago, there was a schoolboy.
    He lived in a cottage by the sea.
And the very first thing he could remember
    Was the rigging of the schooners by the quay.

He could watch them, when he woke, from his window,
    With the tall cranes hoisting out the freight.
And he used to think of shipping as a sea cook,
    And sailing to the Golden Gate.

For he used to buy the yellow penny dreadfuls,
    And read them where he fished for conger eels,
And listened to the lapping of the water,
    The green and oily water round the keels.

There were trawlers with their shark-mouthed flatfish,
    And red nets hanging out to dry,

And the skate the skipper kept because he liked 'em,
  And landsmen never knew the fish to fry.

There were brigantines with timber out of Norroway,
  Oozing with the syrups of the pine.
There were rusty, dusty schooners out of Sunderland,
  And ships of the Blue Cross line.

And to tumble down a hatch into the cabin
  Was better than the best of broken rules;
For the smell of 'em was like a Christmas dinner,
  And the feel of 'em was like a box of tools.

And before he went to sleep in the evening,
  The very last thing that he could see
Was the sailormen a-dancing in the moonlight
  By the capstan that stood upon the quay.

He is perched upon a high stool in London.
  The Golden Gate is very far away.
They caught him, and they caged him, like a squirrel.
  He is totting up accounts, and going gray.

He will never, never, never sail to Frisco.
  But the very last thing that he will see
Will be sailormen a-dancing in the sunrise
  By the capstan that stands upon the quay . . .

To the tune of an old concertina,
  By the capstan that stands upon the quay.

ALFRED NOYES

Babette's Love

BABETTE she was a fisher gal,
    With jupon striped and cap in crimps.
She passed her days inside the Halle,
    Or catching little nimble shrimps.
Yet she was sweet as flowers in May,
With no professional bouquet.

JACOT was, of the Customs bold,
    An officer, at gay Boulogne.
He loved BABETTE—his love he told,
    And sighed, "Oh, soyez vous my own!"
But "Non!" said she, "JACOT, my pet,
Vous êtes trop scraggy pour BABETTE.

"Of one alone I nightly dream,
    An able mariner is he,
And gaily serves the Gen'ral Steam-
    Boat Navigation Companee.
I'll marry him, if he but will—
His name, I rather think, is BILL.

"I see him when he's not aware,
    Upon our hospitable coast,
Reclining with an easy air
    Upon the *Port* against a post,
A-thinking of, I'll dare to say,
His native Chelsea far away!"

"Oh, mon!" exclaimed the Customs bold,
    "Mes yeux!" he said (which means "my eye").
"Oh, chère!" he also cried, I'm told;
    "Par Jove," he added, with a sigh.
"Oh, mon! oh, chère! mes yeux! par Jove!
Je n'aime pas cet enticing cove!"

The *Panther*'s captain stood hard by,
    He was a man of morals strict;
If e'er a sailor winked his eye,
    Straightway he had that sailor licked,
Mastheaded all (such was his code)
Who dashed or jiggered, blessed or blowed.

He wept to think a tar of his
    Should lean so gracefully on posts,
He sighed and sobbed to think of this,

On foreign, French, and friendly coasts.
"It's human natur', p'raps—if so,
Oh, isn't human natur' low!"

He called his BILL, who pulled his curl;
    He said, "My BILL, I understand
You've captivated some young gurl
    On this here French and foreign land.
Her tender heart your beauties jog—
They do, you know they do, you dog.

"You have a graceful way, I learn,
    Of leaning airily on posts,
By which you've been and caused to burn
    A tender flame on these here coasts.
A fisher gurl, I much regret—
Her age, sixteen—her name, BABETTE.

"You'll marry her, you gentle tar—
    Your union I myself will bless,
And when you matrimonied are,
    I will appoint her stewardess."
But WILLIAM hitched himself and sighed,
And cleared his throat, and thus replied:

"Not so: unless you're fond of strife,
    You'd better mind your own affairs,
I have an able-bodied wife
    Awaiting me at Wapping Stairs;
If all this here to her I tell,
She'll larrup you and me as well.

"Skin-deep, and valued at a pin,
 Is beauty such as VENUS *owns*—
Her beauty is beneath her skin,
 And lies in layers on her bones.
The other sailors of the crew
They always calls her 'Whopping Sue!' "

"Oho!" the Captain said, "I see!
 And is she then so very strong?"
"She'd take your honor's scruff," said he,
 "And pitch you over to Bolong!"
"I pardon you," the Captain said,
"The fair BABETTE you needn't wed."

Perhaps the Customs had his will,
 And coaxed the scornful girl to wed,
Perhaps the Captain and his BILL
 And WILLIAM's little wife are dead;
Or p'raps they're all alive and well:
I cannot, cannot, cannot tell.

W. S. GILBERT

The Ballad of *Kon-Tiki*

THE RAFT

All day the plane had searched for them, the wild
Kon-Tiki sailors on their brittle raft,
In vain: circling the world from sea rim to sea rim,
Diving down through the boisterous cloud to find
No land anywhere, no sign of raft
Or any living thing, only
The foam-white wave in a wilderness of water
And a wilderness of hope.

What need of a plane?
It's easier for *you* to find them.
Plunge with me now through the cloud—if you dare—

And with an eagle eye pin-point
One flake of foam darker than the rest.
That's the raft, d'you see it?—tiny, frail
As a rose petal blown on a stormy lake.
Drop closer now. Hover over the wave
Till you feel the sting of salt. It's not so frail
As it looks, that raft. Nine logs of balsa wood
Lashed side to side, pointed
With splashboards at the prow;
For mast two mangrove stems tied at the top;
A bamboo yard with four-corner sail painted
With *Kon-Tiki*'s bearded face, *Kon-Tiki* son of the Sun;
Behind him the cane cabin, plaited with reed
And tiled with banana leaf, a ramshackle tool-shed thing
That creaks in every wind. This was their home
For a hundred days, this wooden tray, this balsa platter,
This cork steam roller snubbing the cheeky wave,
Now riding the mountain crest, now swamped
And swallowed, a sieve to each falling sea.

Six men lived here: the skipper,
Thor Heyerdahl of Norway, who planned the game,
Confident, courageous as the god
Who gave him his name—he's at the helm now,
Tugging at the tiller in the climbing sea;
Torstein Raaby, merry and resourceful,
A wizard in wireless—d'you see him there
Crouched in the corner with earphones plastered
On his yellow stubble hair,
Tapping out a message with battery and box?
(Don't touch him for fear of electric shocks);

And Knut beside him, brave Knut of Norway . . .
Danielsson of Sweden, cook and quartermaster,
Professor with a flaming beard
That seemed to scorch his face, most learned about fish,
Placid in peril—look at him,
Sprawled on the cabin floor with his beard in a book.
He doesn't notice how the raft reels and rocks
But calmly reads on and on and on—
There are seventy more books in his stock;
Herman Watzinger, weather boss and boatswain—
Is there a tougher man alive?
He broke his neck at Lima and survived.
Lastly, Erik Hesselberg, a burly fellow
Broad as a barn door and full of fun,
He was everything rolled into one:
Navigator, splicer, sail-patcher, wood-carver,
Draughtsman and painter, hulking hula dancer—
And he could play the mandolin
And sing:
    "Violée violà violée-li-lillio
    The breadboard's a-bobbing on the wild wet sea
    O the whale and the shark they can nibble her like billy-o
    And swaller all the others—but they won't get me!"
And there was a green parrot in a cage,
A real smarty who with one tweak of his beak
Could twist the doorknob and vanish,
And if you chased him swear at you in Swedish
And in Spanish.
Six men, a parrot, and a small tame crab
Whose name was Johnny; he lived in a hole near the steering block
And came when he was called.

They were not lonely. They found the sea
No barren waste but a living world,
Peopled as the woodland with wild creatures,
Curious and shy. The rough-riding steamer
With his foaming prow and his engine roar
Sees them not. But *Kon-Tiki* scared them not away.
As timid birds at twilight hop and twitter
On the summer lawn about the quiet house,
So now about the noiseless floating raft
The frolicking sea-dwellers. Then did Ocean,
The great showman, out of the bountiful deep
Conjure all manner of strange creatures
To delight them: flying fish that shot through the air
Like quicksilver, smack against the sail,
Then dropped to deck into the breakfast saucepan
Waiting there; the prosperous tunny,
Fat as an alderman with rows of double chins;
The glorious dolphin, bluebottle-green
With glittering golden fins, greedy
For the succulent weed that trailed like garlands
From the steering oar. There were many more—
Take the blue shark, a glutton
For blood; he'd swallow a dolphin, bones and all,
And crunch them like a concrete mixer. They learnt
How to fool him with titbits, to get him
By his tail and haul abroad, skipping
Quickly from the snapping jaw—
He'd make a meal of anyone who let him!
(Rare sport this for the parrot, who
For safety flew to the roof of the raft

And shrieked at the fun of it and laughed and laughed.)
Every kind they saw, from the million pilot fish
Tiny as a fingernail
To the majestic tremendous spotted whale,
Long as a tennis court, who could—
Were he so minded—with one flick of his great tail
Have swatted them flat as a fly. But he couldn't be bothered.
Instead, circling cumbrously below,
He scratched his lazy back on the steering oar,
Till Erik sent him packing
With half a foot of steel in his spine.
Deep down he plunged, and the harpoon line—
Whipping through their hands—snapped like twine.

These marvels were the day's. What words
Can paint the night,
When the sea was no darkness but a universe of light?
Lo, in their wake a shoal
Of little shrimps, all shining,
A sprinkle of red coal!
Drawn by the gleaming cabin lamp, the octopus,
The giant squid with green ghostly eyes,
Hugged and hypnotized;
While, fathoms below, in the pitch-black deep were gliding
Balloons of flashing fire, silver
Streaming meteors. O world of wonder!
O splendid pageantry!
Hour after dreamy hour they gazed spellbound,
Trailing their fingers in the starry sea.

IAN SERRAILLIER

Indexes

Index of Authors

Index of Titles

233

234